Whatever was up there now, moving along slithering sound. It found the wall, slapped wetly against it and started to inch along, making for the bars. Romero was thinking something like a slug here, but big and fleshy and horrible and he didn't know all what. As it pulled itself along the wall, it made faint chirruping noises, clicking sounds like claws or teeth kissing the concrete.

It would ooze forward a moment or two, then pause...as if checking now and then to see if anyone was listening.

Romero was listening, but not moving. For hearing it was one thing, but seeing...no, the idea of that curdled his guts like sour milk.

And then it...leaped through the air, hit the bars with a splattering sound. Romero could hear it breathing, gurgling. In the wan light from the guard's station, he could see something large and shapeless spread out on the bars like a huge, rubbery spider...

FEAR ME

TIM CURRAN

Cover art and design by David Dodd

First Crossroad Press Edition

1

Soon as Romero saw the new meat, he knew there was going to trouble. He felt it down in his guts, something cold and inexplicable that just started chewing through him. You were sitting on ten years hard time and wouldn't see parole for another three, you got real good at spotting trouble. Knowing how it smelled, how it walked, and how it talked.

The sergeant hack, Jorgensen, brought the new meat in, said, "Here you go, Romero, we got you a new cellmate. He's young and pure, don't go dirtying him up." Jorgensen thought that was funny, took the kid by the arm and pushed him at Romero. "He's all yours now, don't break him."

Then Jorgensen stepped out and the cell door slid closed. He went on his merry way, twirling his stick, laughing with the other hacks, looking for cons to hassle and heads to crack.

Romero just stood there, looking over the new meat. This was his second stretch. He'd already done five years at Brickhaven for grand theft and an illegal weapons charge when he was twenty. Now he was forty, doing a dime for aggravated assault and battery of a police officer, staring down the long tunnel at the light flickering at the end. He wanted to feel that light on him really bad, on his face and hands, making things glow inside him where there had only been darkness for too long.

What he didn't need was this skinny little boy fucking things up for him.

"You got a name, Cherry?" Romero put to him, crossing his muscular forearms over his chest, letting the kid see the jailhouse tats on them. Letting him know right off that he was a ballbuster, a hardtimer that would bite out your eyes and fuck your skull if you got in his way.

"Danny, Danny Palmquist," the kid said.

Romero shook his head. Candy-ass name like that. *Palmquist*. Damn, the cons were going to eat that up with their bare hands. "Good, Danny, I'll call you Cherry. You got a problem with that, *Cherry?*"

Little shit didn't say anything. He just stood there in the corner, that lost puppy hang-dog look on his face. But then, Romero knew, that's what guys like Danny Palmquist were: hang-dog puppies.

Jesus, look at the kid.

Not more than 5'6, 5'7, maybe 140 pounds, more meat on a taco than this one. The cons were probably already arm-wrestling to see who got to pop his puppy ass first. Sickening. Just a skinny little nothing. Size didn't always matter—some of the meanest pricks behind those walls were little guys with shivs and acid attitudes—but you could see that Danny Palmquist was a zero. He wouldn't be able to defend himself, which made him prey. Within 48 hours, he was going to be somebody's punk old lady.

Romero was hard.

Before he took this fall, he'd worked the streets, pushed coke and junk, stole cars, busted skulls, even had himself a few bodies out there. A life like that made a guy ready for the joint. Made him lean, mean, ready to bust if you looked at him the wrong way. But this kid? No, he didn't have any streets on him. He was small town, junior glee-club material. Probably pissed himself when the local bully gave him a shove. There was just nowhere for a guy like that in a maximum-security joint. Blacks would sniff out his sugar-ass. If they didn't, spics would take him. Shit, cons his own color—bikers and Aryan Brothers—would be all over him, selling his ass first thing you knew.

He needed somebody to watch over him, protect him.

But he wasn't tough enough for the ABs, Skinheads, or redneck whiteboy traffickers. No gang would touch a cherry like that. And Romero? He had his own problems.

He sat on his bunk, lit a cigarette. "You're on top, Cherry."

But the kid didn't move. "What you in for?" he asked.

Stupid little peckerwood. *What you in for?* Kid saw too many prison movies, James Cagney and shit. "Like I said," Romero told him. "You're on top."

"I guess you don't like to talk much."

Romero gave him the look. "Shut your pisshole, Cherry. You don't, I'll shove something in there, shut it for you. You know what I'm saying to you?"

The kid did.

2

The second day.

The kid was still a virgin and still hadn't been extorted, but it wouldn't last. Out in the yard, all the cons were watching him, smelling that new meat, wondering whose punk he was going to be.

Wasn't going to be long, Romero knew.

First, they'd take his food in the mess hall, then they'd throw him a beating out in the yard, maybe try to rape him in the laundry or showers. That's how it would begin. Pressure would build. Cons would get randy like starving dogs circling a fresh, juicy bone. Wondering who was going to get the first bite. Then some ballbuster would come along, tell Palmquist that he'd protect him for money. Didn't matter where he got it—mother, father, sister, brother, priest—long as he got it. And if he couldn't get it? Then he'd be a punk for some hardtimer, sucking the guy's dick and bending over for him. Because that's how it worked inside: You weren't part of a gang or tough enough to do your own fighting, somebody had to do it for you.

And it never came free.

Not at Shaddock Valley.

It was a real hard-time sort of hole. You locked up thousands of guys like animals for months and years, pretty soon even the good ones lost their humanity and showed their teeth. It was a grim, gray concrete world where you buried hope with the biggest shovel you could find and yourself with it. Violent guards, bad food, cramped conditions, loneliness, frustration. Hot in the summer, like an icebox in the winter. Bugs. Rats. Throw into the mix dehumanizing treatment and the constant invasion of privacy, the degradation of strip searches and cavity searches…it took away what was left. Then all you had were predators and prey. Guys with tattoos and dead eyes wandering the yard, sniffing around the block, looking for the stragglers, the weak ones, anything they could bring down, sink their teeth into that wouldn't bite back.

The inmates at Shaddock robbed each other, fought each other, pushed drugs and booze, smuggled porno and contraband, sometimes even women. They killed for money and sometimes for free. They made weapons and stabbed each other, beat each other, raped each other, murdered each other, snitched on each other. Most of them had absolutely nothing to lose. Shaddock was a bubbling, seething cauldron flavored by the very worst society had to offer—bullies and rapists, serial killers and racists, Jesus freaks and gangsters, psychopaths and fanatics—only in there it was compressed, localized, compacted behind barbwire and high stone walls. Refined, if you will, into a toxic brew that stank like shit and body odor, vomit and pain and blackness and you could smell it the moment they processed you through.

End of the line.

And in such a place, a guy like Danny Palmquist didn't stand a chance.

3

"You don't say much do you?"

Romero was laying on his bunk before lights out, trying to read a book about some guy surviving in Antarctica. He liked books like that because he understood survival very very well. "Why don't you shut the fuck up, Cherry?"

The kid sighed, sitting at the little desk against the cement block wall, staring at those bars. "Just saying, shit, we're locked up together, might as well pass the time."

"Listen, Cherry. I ain't trying to get in your asshole or slit your throat...why don't you be happy with that?"

"I'm just saying we could talk."

Romero didn't want that, didn't want nothing to do with the little bastard. You talked to a guy, then you started feeling like he was your friend. And when that happened, you felt like you had to take care of him.

And I don't need that, he thought, *I really don't.*

Thing was, Romero wasn't sure that this is what was bothering him about the kid. That he'd have to fight his battles for him. There was something else, something about the kid he just didn't like only he wasn't sure what it was.

"Okay, Cherry, give it to me then. Tell me your sad fucking story. What did you do? Rape somebody's poodle? Go after a couple kids? Tell me the kind of pathetic shit that landed you here."

"Manslaughter."

Romero almost laughed. *Manslaughter?* "You? What'd you do? Run down some old lady in your mommy's car?"

Palmquist wasn't biting. "No...there was a girl. We were sort of going out, you know? Nothing major. Just some dates and things. She got killed, murdered, and they blamed me for it because I was the last one with her." The kid studied his hands, maybe wondering if they were capable of doing what the courts charged him with. "So...I don't know, I copped a plea. Took five years for manslaughter, otherwise the DA wanted to prosecute me for capital murder."

Romero did laugh now. "Why the fuck you do that, Cherry? DA was just dancing, you stupid shit, bobbing and weaving. They try you for murder one, they got to prove it."

"My lawyer said that, too, but I went for it."

"You should've listened to him, Cherry. You'd be out there now."

But Palmquist just shook his head. "No, you don't understand. I didn't kill that girl, my brother did. And, well, I didn't want any of that coming out."

Romero chuckled, lit a cigarette. "That's some kind of brother you got there, letting you do time for him."

"My brother...Damon...he's not like us, he's different. I didn't want it coming out about the way he was, the things he does."

Romero just watched Danny Palmquist, Cherry sonofabitch. Way he talked, you would have thought this brother of his swung from trees, had two heads, and a stainless-steel dick. It was all pretty funny in a seriously fucked up sort

7

of way. When the kid talked about his brother, he got a real skittish look in his eyes like maybe he was afraid of him. Maybe that's what this was all about.

Romero said, "You better screw your head on straight, Cherry. And you better do it soon. Get hold of your lawyer, tell him the truth. It's what you gotta do."

"I can't do that."

"Then you're gonna suffer, Cherry. You're gonna suffer real bad."

The kid looked at him now, a dusting of menace in his eyes. "I ain't a cherry, Romero. This is the second joint I've been in. I know how things work."

"Yeah? Where were you before?"

"Brickhaven, upstate."

"Brickhaven?"

"Sure. You been there?"

Romero told him he had, years before.

Brickhaven. Is that what the kid said? Brickhaven was definitely no kiddie joint. He couldn't imagine this fish surviving in a place like that. Maybe he got lucky, but he wouldn't get lucky at Shaddock Valley. Shaddock got all the troublemakers who couldn't make it in the other state joints. But it all gave Romero pause...something had happened at Brickhaven a few months before, something real ugly, and he was starting to wonder now how the kid might have factored into that business.

"Brickhaven ain't Shaddock, Cherry. Guys in here'll do bad things to you."

"Worse than they did to me at Brickhaven?"

"Yes."

But Palmquist just shook his head. "They better not. Not if they know what's good for 'em...my brother finds out, it'll be trouble."

"In *here?* You stupid little shit! Listen to yourself. Your brother can't help you in here. Don't you see that? Maybe he's some kind of crazy-assed freak out in the world, but in here you're on your own."

Palmquist's eyes went about three shades darker, looked like bubbling sap. "You better watch it, Romero. You don't want to piss him off."

Romero tossed his cigarette and got to his feet. "Fuck you say, asshole? Fuck you think you're talking to, motherfucker?" Romero was standing over him now, ready to bust him, slap that cherry face right off the bone beneath. "Let's tell it the way it is, Cherry. How about we do that? Maybe you survived Brickhaven, maybe you got lucky, but you won't get lucky in here. You're nothing but meat and everyone wants a bite, tasty thing like you. These animals will stab you, beat you, burn you, rape you. And who's gonna stop 'em? This fuck-up dog-humping brother of yours? Don't make me fucking laugh. This is the end of the world, you dumb cocksucker."

Palmquist looked like he was ready to cry.

And Romero wanted him to. It was the best thing that could happen to him, drain all that human weakness right out of him, squeeze the little prick dry and the sooner the better. "I'm gonna let you in on a little secret, Cherry. You don't stand a chance. You might as well pick your daddy now before he picks you."

"Hell, I will."

Romero wanted to put his hands on him, give him some pain to think about…but it was there again, that feeling in his guts, that sense that this kid was trouble, three kinds of hell. It stayed Romero's hands…the idea of touching him was somehow *loathsome*, like handling a big spider or a dead rat crawling with worms. A deep-set almost physical revulsion.

9

And feeling that the kid had that kind of power over him when he had no damn right to, just pissed Romero off. "You goddamn punk! Right now, I decide to beat you or rape your ass, you can't stop me. I'll take what I want and ain't nothing you can do about it, is there? I'll beat you and fuck you and tomorrow or next week, I'll be selling your sweet ass for cigarettes and soap. You like that? *You like that idea?* Why don't you gimme a fucking reason, Cherry, gimme a reason to pull my razor and cut you to shreds and fuck what's left. Go ahead, you fucking little snot, *gimme a reason…*"

But Palmquist didn't.

He just stared at those bars like he was wondering what was beyond them.

4

The next morning, out in the yard.

Romero was there with a Hispanic strong-arm thief named JoJo Aquintez and a big, tattooed biker named Riggs who looked like something that sharpened its teeth on bones in a Neolithic cave. All three of them, sitting on a picnic table near the wall, looked outrageous in their orange prison-issue jumpsuits.

Riggs was saying how he was walking in four months, his term would be up. He had waved his right to parole, did the extra time so he wouldn't have no parole officer sniffing around his ass out in the world.

"I walk through them fucking gates, boys, I walk high and free," he told them. "Start turning some green day one."

Romero knew what that was about.

Riggs was a member of the Mongols motorcycle club, a major player in their meth distribution network. When he got out, he was just going to pick up where he left off. Most cons were like that. Riggs had pulled a nickel for putting a black cocaine dealer in a wheelchair with his bare hands. That's the sort of guy he was.

Aquintez was saying how he'd be staring at those walls for some time to come, had five more years to pull on his bit. But when he got out, no more armed robbery. That's what got him here. He was thinking something less violent, maybe insurance fraud. Guy could make a killing at that, if he knew the angles.

Romero wasn't listening, though.

He was watching Danny Palmquist hanging around over there by the baseball diamond with all the other losers—the child molesters and rapists, serial killers and weaklings. The other cons didn't like those types, guys that hurt kids and women. It didn't take any balls for that. And in stir, real balls carried respect, carried dignity, assured your place in the food chain as a real man. Even in prison there were undesirables, guys you could look down on. Sometimes, when the real cons were having a hard day, they'd go over there to the diamond and kick the shit out of some faggot serial killer or short-eye. Made them feel better about themselves.

That's where Palmquist was.

Keeping to himself, trying to avoid the attentions of the baby-rapers over there.

But some of the cons in the yard were watching him, wondering about the new bitch, thinking about running his track.

"What you think of your new cellie, Romero?" Aquintez asked, pulling off a home-rolled cigarette, half-tobacco and half-Mary Jane.

Good question, that one. Thing was, Romero just wasn't sure. Kid was a punk, he was meat, harmless as a kitty in a box…yet, *yet* there was something creepy about the little bastard. Something Romero didn't care for, but couldn't honestly put a name to.

"Look where he's hanging at," Romero said. "What's that tell you?"

Riggs shook his head, had half a mind to waltz over there and kick some rapo ass.

"Just a punk," Romero said. "Ain't nothing more than that."

"I hear he was over at Brickhaven, heard he got into some trouble there," Aquintez mentioned. "Can't seem to find out what he did, though."

"Look at him," Riggs said in his gravelly voice. "He was probably somebody's old lady over there. Maybe he fell in love with some punk and his daddy took it personal."

Romero said, "He's loony, that one. Thinks if anyone throws down on him, his brother's gonna come save his white meat ass."

Aquintez thought that was funny. "Gonna break in or what? Never heard of a guy breaking into Shaddock. Out once or twice, but never in."

"Brickhaven," Riggs said, scratching his shaggy beard. "That was some funny shit happened there. I knew one of them guys that got done. His name was Fritz, Donnie Fritz. A real nasty piece of work. Him and his cellie, some nigger named Boles...shit, they got done after lock-down, done real bad."

And that was the word coming down the prison grapevine. Fritz and Boles got murdered in their cells, looked like somebody had taken a chainsaw after them. Nothing but a lot of meat and blood to mark their passing. And after lock-down, yet. That was hard to explain.

"Maybe you want a new cellie," Aquintez told Romero. "I'll talk to Benny, he can square it for you."

But Romero shook his head. "Not yet. This kid is funny, something odd about him. I wanna see how it plays out."

At the baseball diamond, a big black guy name of Reggie Weems was getting tired of waiting. He went over there and all the other rapos got out of his way. He went right up to Palmquist, took hold of him and brought the little shit up real close like he was going to kiss him. There was a scuffle and Weems started knocking the kid around.

"Looks like your boy got a bite with that bait he's been trolling," Aquintez said, unconcerned.

Riggs laughed, thought it was funny Weems knocking the shit out of that little weasel.

Romero tossed his cigarette, started over there, not really sure why.

Aquintez said, "Fuck you going? He your punk or what? I don't know, home, that Weems is a rough one, you better take a blade. Do it proper."

But Romero didn't want a blade and he didn't want Riggs's help either. The biker said he'd come, that he could handle Weems just fine. But Romero told them he just wanted to watch Palmquist get a dose of reality.

By the time he got there, it was over with.

The hacks hadn't seen a thing. Partly because the other cons ringed Weems and Palmquist in so they could dance in private and partly because the hacks never saw anything. You could gang rape their mothers three feet away and they wouldn't put down their magazines to stop it. Lazy, stupid, and indifferent were a way of life for hacks, Romero knew.

Weems was already moving off to join the brothers over by the basketball courts. He didn't pay no mind to Romero and Romero paid no mind to him. Palmquist was sitting on his ass, spitting out blood and teeth. His left eye was beginning to swell shut and his lower lip was almost ripped from his mouth.

"You like that?" Romero put to him, not bothering to offer him a hand or even a squirt of sympathy. "Well, you better get used to it, Cherry. Because you're gonna be living on a steady diet of ass-beatings twenty-four/seven. Every day from now on. First, they're going to beat you, then...you know what comes next, don't you?"

Palmquist nodded. "I know. I been here before, in this situation."

Romero figured some con had busted his ass at Brickhaven. Wouldn't have surprised him. "Well, then you know what you're in for."

But Palmquist just shook his head. "That fucking nigger is dead, only he don't know it yet and there ain't shit I can do about it." He was grinning now, blood all over his teeth. "See, Romero, I got me an ace in the hole."

"You're gonna have more than an ace in there, mark my word," Romero said.

But Palmquist said nothing.

5

L ater that afternoon, Riggs passed the word to Romero that Black Dog wanted to see him. It wasn't good. Anytime Black Dog was involved it just couldn't be a good thing.

Black Dog was a patched blood member of the Hell's Angels and one of the Filthy Few, which was the enforcement wing of the Angels who beat, mauled, and murdered any that violated club policies or encroached on their lucrative drug turf. He was absolutely fearless, tough, and merciless. He had a psychotic volatile temper and a reputation for bloodshed and violence that few could match behind those walls. He was sitting on a seventy-five-year stretch for murder conspiracy.

"Hell's he want?' Romero asked.

But Riggs just shrugged. "Can't say, my brother. He reached out through us because he wants a sit-down with you."

By "us" Riggs meant the Mongols. There had been blood wars between the Angels and Mongols on the outside, but behind the walls at Shaddock, they kept an uneasy truce.

Romero found Black Dog over at the iron pile, bench-pressing the sort of weight that would have driven most men into the ground. He finished, mopping sweat from his face with

16

his t-shirt. "Romero," he said. "Glad you came. We need to talk."

Romero sighed, lit a cigarette. "I'm listening."

"It's about your cellie," Blackdog said. "That fish Palmquist. I need to know what your intentions are."

"Intentions?"

Black Dog nodded. "Some shit happened at Brickhaven. You probably heard. Your fish was involved in that, somehow, some way. Was a dude over there, Donnie Fritz, he got done. Some people think your fish had a hand in it."

Romero laughed. "Palmquist? We talking about the same guy?"

"We are."

"This kid ain't got it in him, Dog."

"Some people think different."

"Then some people are full of shit."

"Go easy, man, go easy here."

Even to Romero, Blackdog was fearsome. He stood an easy 6'6 and weighed 300 pounds and there was not a scrap of fat on him. His body was covered in prison tattoos and many of them, if you knew how to read them, told the story of who he was and where he'd been, the things he'd done and the bodies he'd left in his wake. One each huge bulging bicep there was an immense blood-red swastika.

He was not a man to cross.

Black Dog was not elaborating on these "people," at least not yet. And knowing him and his connections it could have been anybody from the Italians to the Mexicans, his biker brothers or the ABs. Take your pick.

"Listen, Dog," Romero said, standing his ground. "Palmquist is meat. He's harmless. There's no way he did someone like Fritz. Besides, way I hear it, Fritz and his cellie got done after lock-down. Now how the fuck could the fish be involved in that?"

Black Dog thought about that.

Even with the proper schooling, Romero doubted that Palmquist would ever make a good con. He'd never have the nuts to stand up for himself and that made him a victim, plain and simple.

When Romero was a young punk at Brickhaven, after he'd been processed into the general population, an old timer named Skip Hannaway came up to him and asked him what the state had sent him away to college for. Romero told him about the thing he had for stealing cars.

"Let me tell you how things work here, son," Skip said. "Everything that happens in a hard-time joint revolves around fear and anger. These are the only two emotions you will encounter in this cesspool. The primary motivations behind everything. You got to learn how to control fear and use anger. It's the only way to survive. Anybody gives you shit, you give it back in spades. You make that fucker wish he'd never been born. A pipe is a good thing. You see somebody coming at you, break 'em with it. Lay it upside their head, crack their kneecaps with it, break their hands. Let 'em all know that you have a wild, insane temper and they'll keep away. Most cons are cowards. They like to come up behind you, throw you a beating or stick a knife in you when your back's turned. Not too many of them will do it face to face and that's because they don't want to get hurt. You show 'em pain, let 'em see their own blood…you'll be surprised how meek they become."

Good advice that Romero put into play his second day there when some old pervert made a play for him.

But Palmquist?

No, he just didn't have it in him.

He'd never make it.

Life in the joint was indifferent hacks and crowding, dehumanizing conditions and shitty food. You shivered in your bunk in the winter and sweated and stank in the summer. You tried to keep the flies off your face and the lice out of your hair and the rats from biting your feet while you slept. Some perv made a play for your asshole, you beat him. Some con tried to extort you or slide a shank into you when your back was turned, you crippled them.

Politics.

That's all it came down to: politics.

And Palmquist would never be able to play the game.

"Listen to me, Romero. Hear what I say. Donnie Fritz was hooked up with some big players. They didn't take kindly to what happened at The Brick and they want payback. They want the fish to suffer," Black Dog explained. "Now I saw you today. When Weems went after your boy, it looked like you were thinking about intervening. Not good. You laying claim to the fish as your boy?"

"No."

"That's good. See, those friends of Fritz's, they reached out to Papa Joe…"

Shit. Papa Joe was Joseph Scallati, an incarcerated heroin trafficker and a made guy in the mob. When he had your number, there was no hole deep enough to hide in. He had deep pockets and the cons *and* hacks were eating out of his hands. He had not only the Italians standing behind him, but the biker gangs he used for muscle and the Latin gangs that were lorded over by the Mexican Mafia. And if that wasn't enough, he also had the Aryan Brotherhood.

The ABs were the most ruthless and savage white prison gang ever formed. They had begun during the race riots at San Quentin during the '60s and had carved themselves an especially bloodthirsty niche ever since. At Quentin, the ABs had a standing "kill on sight" order and they murdered every black they found. In the years since, it had mellowed somewhat, but they were still unbelievably violent and dangerous. Unlike most prison gangs who relied on strength in numbers, the ABs had a blood in, blood out rule: in other words, you had to kill someone to get in and only death could get you out. Even outside prison walls, the gang was involved in organized crime, a narcotics conduit for their imprisoned brothers.

The bikers were bad enough, but these guys were fanatics.

Romero didn't want to see Palmquist victimized and broken...but he couldn't stand up against something like this.

"So, you see how things stand," Black Dog said.

"I guess I do."

Black Dog nodded. "Just wanted you to get this word of advice and look the other way. Papa Joe's sending Tony Gordo after him and you don't want to get involved in that shit."

Romero felt sick to his stomach.

Tony Gordo was a mob enforcer who was doing two consecutive life terms for murder. A big, evil piece of work, the sort of scavenger only the streets could produce. Just a human monster that had been feeding off the bloated body of a diseased society since the very moment his eyes flicked opened in that death mask he called a face. That was Gordo. Tipping the scales at 400 pounds, he was just shy of seven feet tall and a born monster. Nobody liked him, but the Italians used him for muscle. Gordo's biggest joy in life was sodomizing the new fish. Black, white, didn't matter, if you had a hole in your backside then it was his duty to fill it. He started with beatings which were like foreplay to him that led up to the violent act of consummation.

"So, Papa Joe is going to let that fucking freak have his fun?"

Black Dog shrugged. "Ain't none of us like it, but it's business. Strictly business. You ain't sweet on the fish, are you?"

Romero didn't answer that one.

He walked away. He couldn't trust what his mouth might say and what kind of shit it might get him into. Palmquist's ticket was already punched. The hacks wouldn't help him and nobody in the joint would dare intervene in Papa Joe's business and especially with a meat-eater like Gordo involved.

Bunching his fists, frustrated and pissed-off, Romero began to wonder what he was going to do about it. Was he going to be smart and look the other way or was he going to jump feet-first into the fires of hell?

The thing was, he didn't really know.

6

L ights out.
Romero was lying on his bunk, thinking and trying not
to. There were a lot of things flying around in his head, a real
shitstorm is what it was. He was thinking about the kid, about
Palmquist, thinking how it was going to be for the little bastard
when Reggie Weems and his crew started turning up the heat,
started making these beatings a daily thing. How it was going
to be when they all started using him, passing him around like
a five-dollar hooker in a lumber camp. Because that's where this
trail always led. The kid was in for it. Maybe he already had a
taste at Brickhaven, but it was going to be worse here.

Things were always worse at Shaddock.

Romero had seen it before and it always made him sick. Sick
to watch some kid putting up with that, his dignity stripped
away from him day by miserable day until there wasn't
anything left when those animals were through. Until
Palmquist was a pale, trembling thing, a bitch that only spoke
when spoken to, that would suck dick or spread his cheeks
anytime some lifer snapped his oily fingers.

Romero couldn't get involved.

22

He got in Weems' way and there was going to be trouble. And it could only end one way, with Romero shanking him, stabbing that dumb fucking spade until he bled out. And if Romero did that, he made that choice, one of Weems' crew would rat on him. See to it that he was sitting here at Shaddock Valley for another ten or twenty years. Jesus. The idea of that made Romero's throat squeeze tight until he could barely fill his lungs with air. But to watch Palmquist go like that…

Reggie Weems is going to be the least of that kid's worries and you know it, now that Papa Joe is putting Tony Gordo on him. Even if the kid slips away from Weems, there's no way in hell he'll get away from that fucking monster.

Romero had done his share of time. But never in all those years did humping somebody's ass seem like a good alternative. If it was that bad on you, you used your hand. But some of these guys, they liked it just fine, the sex you could get here in prison.

So, you're just going to let them degrade that kid, aren't you? a voice of guilt hammered at him, just when he'd thought it was long dead. A con with a conscience of all crazy things. *Let them turn him into their whore, break him wide open, tear his soul right out…and you're just going to stand back and let it happen?*

Romero didn't know.

He didn't know much of anything these days.

So, he shut his eyes and tried not to see Reggie Weems or Tony Gordo. He let sleep take him, because tomorrow was just another day like this one and the one two years ago and the one two years from now. Day by day by pissing day, it never changed when you were doing time.

You hardened your heart and bleached your soul white and just looked the other way. It was the only way to get by.

23

7

Romero woke and he had no idea what time it was.
It was just late.

And dark.

Something was going on and he wasn't sure what the hell it could be, but it was real or otherwise it wouldn't have woken him. He listened. Heard his own breathing, the kid's above him. But something else, too, something that made his throat go dry and the flesh at his scalp go tight and hot. It was a funny wet sort of sound, all squishy and slimy-sounding like something was being pulled out of a drain with a coat hanger.

The springs above him creaked ever so slightly and Palmquist shifted up there...only Romero could still hear him breathing deep and long. He was thinking that whatever was moving up there...it wasn't the kid. He didn't know what it was, but he could hear it sliding around with a moist unpleasant sound like a baby crawling free of afterbirth.

Jesus...those sounds...what the hell is happening up there?

Romero figured he didn't want to know, because whatever it was, it was just plain bad, something you just didn't want to look on. The air had gone hot and dank with a gassy odor like rotting cabbage and he was gripping the edges of his bunk as if

24

he was on a rollercoaster and was afraid the car might tip him out at any moment. It was a wild ride and his guts were slicked with cold jelly, his eyes wide and sightless in the darkness. He was thinking about that homemade knife behind the radiator…but he didn't dare go for it, didn't dare make a sound.

Didn't want what was up there to *hear* him.

So, he lay there, stiff as a plank, his muscles bunched and his nerve endings jangling like Christmas bells, a scream lodged in his throat.

More movement.

Whatever was up there with the kid, it was in motion now, moving along the bunk with a stealthy, slithering sound. It found the wall, slapped wetly against it and started to inch along, making for the bars. Romero was thinking something like a slug here, but big and fleshy and horrible and he didn't know all what. As it pulled itself along the wall, it made faint chirruping noises, clicking sounds like claws or teeth kissing the concrete.

It would ooze forward a moment or two, then pause…as if checking now and then to see if anyone was listening.

Romero was listening, but not moving. For hearing it was one thing, but seeing…no, the idea of that curdled his guts like sour milk.

And then it…*leaped* through the air, hit the bars with a splattering sound. Romero could hear it breathing, gurgling. In the wan light from the guard's station, he could see something large and shapeless spread out on the bars like a huge, rubbery spider, contorting boneless limbs spread out in every direction. It was shuddering and pulsing, taking its time. Romero squeezed his eyes shut. He could not look at that thing any longer. He told himself it was a nightmare and the thing was just some nebulous horror that had crawled alive and kicking from one of his childhood dreams.

25

And then…it was gone.

It went right through the bars with a sound like bacon grease dropped in a bucket or mush stirred with a spoon.

Romero was shaking, sweating, doing everything he could not to piss himself or vent that scream buried in his throat. He lay there, trying to catch his breath, wiping perspiration from the gutters under his eyes. Above him, Palmquist was dead asleep, breathing deep and even, lost to the world.

Romero started to think all kinds of awful things, but none of it made a lick of sense and his mind was full of shit and he wondered, really wondered, if maybe he could have dreamt it all.

Part of him latched onto that, told him in an authoritative, reasonable voice that, yes, of course it was a dream…what else could it have been?

About twenty minutes later, though, somebody started screaming.

And the screams…they didn't last long at all.

8

Of course, the prison came alive.

Sometimes you heard screams at night, guys getting shanked or raped and sometimes it was just some con losing his mind, cracking up from the solitude and the cage they kept him in and dozens of things you would never really know about. His mind would go to sauce and he'd start thrashing around, throwing himself at the walls and biting the bars and tossing his shit at anyone that got near like a monkey in a carnival pen.

Sergeant Warres was in charge of the hacks on the graveyard shift and he came up the stairs to D Block, looking pissed-off and anxious to break some skulls with the stick he was swinging at his hip. He was on his walkie-talkie, wanting to know what in the name of Jesus H. Jumping Clusterfucking Christ was going on up there. He cut some orders straight away over his box and his guards did their thing, told the cons to shut their mother-raping, cunting mouths and go to sleep or the lot of them would be thrown in the hole.

It worked and D Block got real quiet, even though everyone knew that there were only thirty Ad-Seg cells to be had. Administrative Segregation, politically correct title, was where guys went when they got out of line and sometimes even when

27

they didn't. It was a nasty, dark, buggy place. And if you thought you'd been alone a lot in your life, you had no conception of what real solitude was until you were locked down in the damp, crawling darkness by yourself.

But it worked and Warres came down the corridor, ignoring his guard's request to turn on the big lights. Security lights were fine, he figured. They were spaced every fifty feet and dim, so that the block corridors were thick with shadows. But that didn't bother Warres, for once the switch was thrown and those doors were shut, nobody got out of their cells...except on the late, late show.

Houle was down there. He was one of the newbies and he looked just as green as frog shit, pale and sweating and about half out of his mind. Warres passed by all those cons pressed up against the bars of their cages, bulging white eyes in black faces and shining red eyes in white faces and damn, he'd never seen them looking so scared before. All the tough-guy, hardass con bullshit had dried up like a pond.

These guys were scared shitless.

Warres got up to Houle, said, "What do you got?"

Houle could barely get a word out without gasping. "Don't go in there, Sarge...Jesus, Weems...I think it's Weems...he's all ripped apart..."

The cell door was open and in his flashlight beam, Warres could see something wet and dark slicked on the bars, a puddle of it coming out under the door. He sucked in a breath and put his light in there, almost screamed himself. Weems looked like a pillow that had its stuffing scattered in every conceivable direction. His insides were on the floor, smeared on the walls, dripping from the ceiling.

His head was bobbing in the shitter, eyes wide and glistening in the flashlight beam.

Weems' cellie, a skinny black guy everyone called Porker, was kneeling on his bed, the top bunk, holding himself and shaking, completely out of his mind. There was blood on him and bits of tissue. He was shivering and sobbing and whispering something no one else could hear.

Enough.

"All right," Warres said. He got on his walkie-talkie. "We got an incident down here…"

9

After the scream, Romero did not get back to sleep. He lay there like the rest of the inmates, bunched and tense and holding his breath, thinking about things that made his flesh crawl. There was electricity feeding through him, as it was probably feeding through everyone on D, like a wire had been stuck up his ass.

But Romero wasn't like the others.

He knew things and maybe he did not know at all. He'd heard that scream just fine, high and sharp and cut short as if something wet had been stuffed in its owner's mouth.

So, he lay there until things began to die down and a silence that was heavy and thick lay over the prison. Around that time, he heard something slither back through the bars and smelled the hot, yeasty stink of rancid fermentation. Palmquist started to moan and thrash.

Sometime later, he began to cry in his sleep.

Or maybe it was Romero himself.

10

Next day, it was all you heard about.
    Didn't matter where you were or whom you were with, the topic of conversation was always the same. The prison became a rumor mill and awful, unbelievable stories began to circulate in that close, sullen atmosphere like disease germs, infecting anyone with a set of ears. Some of the stories were darkly humorous, others like something yanked out of a horror comic or a campfire ghost story. But they kept making the rounds, from the carpentry shop to the craftshop, the mattress factory to the library and the metal shop where license plates were stamped out.

And it was funny, but all the groups and gangs that hated each other on sight, mellowed incrementally, seemed to realize that they were all in the same boat together, running the same risk of sinking in the night like Reggie Weems. Sometimes, a common enemy or common fear could do wonders at a place like Shaddock Valley.

Out in the yard that afternoon, Romero was sitting with his usual bunch—Riggs and Aquintez, a few Latin gangsters and white criminals that had been around the block a long time— discussing the shit, sifting fact from fantasy whenever possible.

31

But it all kept circling back like buzzards on the trail of roadkill: what had happened to Weems was a lot like what had happened to those cons over at Brickhaven. And that got a guy to thinking, making connections where there weren't any or where they were strung so thick they'd trip you right up.

Romero's crew was joined by a shifty, bearded black guy in a wool hat called Beaks because of his sharp, Roman nose. Beaks was doing all-day for murdering his wife and her lover while he was on a coke binge: life without parole. Beaks was locked in the cell across the corridor from Reggie Weems, so people were listening to what he had to say.

"Heard that scream, fuck yes, *shit*...how could you not heard it? Weems...motherfucker was screaming like something was tearing his balls off. Never did hear nothing like that before." Beaks pulled off his cigarette, watching some cons playing a game of pick-up in the distance. "Weems, shit, ya'll know Weems, big ape-ugly motherfucker what ate his meat raw...I thought right away, somebody was in there, got to him. Shit, but you know that motherfucker, nobody play tag with his black ass."

"What'd you see?" Aquintez wanted to know.

"It was dark and shit over there, but I heard something, something wet and sliding...I don't know what the fuck it was...making funny-ass sounds or something, squealing or hissing or some such shit. That's what I hear first and I think: Shit, what the fuck going down over there? Then Weems lets go with that scream. Man, it was crazy hoodoo bullshit, way I'm remembering it."

And that was as close as he could get to it.

In the joint, murders were commonplace. Guys got shanked or piped, thrown off railings or had their food laced with Decon. Now and again, you had something more creative like an electrocution or what was known as a "down-home barbecue": gas dumped through the bars while some con was in lock-up, his cell and himself drenched with the stuff, then a match tossed in there.

But what the forensic team that went into Cell #17, Weems' cell, found was unpleasant even for a prison killing. More than unpleasant, but vicious and psychotic and unexplainable. Houle, the hack who first found Weems, said he'd been ripped apart, mutilated, but that didn't begin to cover it. He had been dismembered and eviscerated, his bowels strung around the cell like streamers of crepe at a kiddy party. His spinal column had actually been pulled out of his back, his head severed but not before his genitals were sheared free and shoved so far down his throat the pathologist had to open his esophagus to get them out. And that was only part of it. Besides the blood and macerated organs, some of Weems' bones had been yanked through the skin and were riddled with teeth marks.

And then there was Porker, Weems' cellmate.

They had to shoot him full of Thorazine and take him out in a straitjacket. The entire time he was babbling and moaning and whimpering crazy shit about "monsters" and "things that looked like people without bones". He was taken to the state hospital that morning for intensive psychotherapy.

"All I know for sure, man," Beaks said to them, "is that something got in there, something I don't want to be thinking about. Whatever it was and whatever the fuck it wanted, they had to take Weems' ass out in bags and buckets, had to mop the floor to get the rest of him."

Romero listened and didn't say a thing.

But he was thinking plenty.

11

Romero was sitting alone in the bleachers by the football field when Aquintez showed. "Hey, home, been looking for you."

"Lot of people seem to be looking for me."

"That's what I hear," Aquintez said. "Word's out that Black Dog warned you off Palmquist."

"Sure, they're saving him for Tony Gordo. Don't want me interfering, doing anything impractical like trying to help the kid out."

He shared his conversation with Black Dog, though Aquintez had pretty much guessed the lay of it. That was prison life: nothing new behind those walls, just the same old games played year in and year out.

Aquintez pulled off his unfiltered cigarette, spitting out a few stray bits of tobacco. "All right, home. I want you to listen to me and hear me on this. You can't stand up against these people. You can't throw yourself against the might of animals like Black Dog and the bikers, the ABs and Papa Joe. They'll fucking skin you, bro."

"I know that, JoJo."

"Then why we having this convo, eh?" Aquintez asked. "Why am I seeing something in your eyes that looks like suicide? Why am I thinking you're just crazy enough to try and protect that fish and forfeit your own life at the same time?"

But Romero would not and maybe *could* not answer that one. Maybe he didn't know himself. All these lean, hungry years just getting by, just existing in this cage, not caring, not giving a damn, getting real slick and practiced at turning a blind eye...and now this. Now something he could not understand had been activated just south of his soul and he could not get a handle on it. It told him he had to help the fish regardless of the consequences.

It would not listen to reason.

It would not be practical.

It refused apathy at every turn.

"There's your boy," Aquintez said, scoping out Palmquist over by the fence, trying to fade away and blend in like a stain on a wall. "There's your fish."

"He ain't mine," Romero told him.

Aquintez exhaled smoke through his nostrils, then he smiled. "Ah, but you're feeling bad for him and the ugly fate awaiting him, eh? Something in you—probably that part I love and respect—wants to protect this kid, beat down any of these vermin who come after him. But you gotta be practical, my friend. Papa Joe says you're going over, you're going over. You stand in the way...bad, very bad. It don't have to be Black Dog's people or the ABs or Papa Joe's social club, he throws the casheesh out there and every con with a shank'll be coming after you. You can't fight that."

"No."

"But you're considering it..."

Romero did not deny that because he couldn't. Part of him very badly wanted to stand up for Palmquist before those animals got their dirty hands all over him...but another part wanted to distance himself from the fish as much as possible. Because there was no getting around one thing much as he tried—Weems had fucked with the kid and now Weems was dead. Something had happened last night. Something when Palmquist was sleeping and Romero could tell himself again and again that he had dreamed it, but he just didn't believe it.

He kept thinking about what Palmquist had said about that brother of his. Crazy shit. It made no sense, yet Romero could not stop thinking about it.

My brother...Damon...he's not like us, he's different.

Ah, it was nonsense. Goddamn fish probably wasn't right in the head. He'd been victimized at Brickhaven and he wasn't in touch with reality, threading the needle in fantasy la-la land. That had to be it.

"But something got Weems," he said under his breath, but loud enough for Aquintez to hear.

"That's true enough, home."

"Bodies keep turning up around Palmquist. Cons are slaughtered in locked cells. Cons that seem to be hooked up with the kid in some way." Romero shook his head. "I'm thinking out loud like some kind of headcase."

"You ain't thinking nothing I'm not, bro," Aquintez said, standing up and butting his cigarette. "Maybe the fish got something going on, eh? Maybe he got a guardian angel. Maybe Tony Gordo ought to think about that."

Romero watched him walk away, thinking pretty much the same things. The problem was that guys like Tony Gordo did not think. They acted, they reacted. Like dumb animals. They were hungry, they ate. They were tired, they slept. You cornered them, they clawed out your eyes. And when their hormones got the best of them, they—

36

"Hey, Romero," one of the hacks said, motioning with his stick. "You got cigarette butts on the ground. Clean it up. Don't be messing up my fucking yard."

"Yes sir, boss," Romero said.

12

That evening, in C-block rec room, a child molester named Neil Givens was hiding out in a darkened corner reading his Bible, trying to figure out a way to make God forgive him for violating one of his lambs.

"The way I understand it," he said in a low voice, "is that we are brought unto this earth imperfect and therefore, we sin."

A skinny black kid named Skiv, nodded his head without looking up from his magazine. "If you say so."

Every day at Shaddock Valley was the same for Givens. Hour after hour, hoping, praying he would not be noticed by the other cons that came and went. Today, he had been successful. None of the usual toughs baited him, noticed him, or even insulted him. Nothing.

Like he was invisible.

Did not exist.

And that was oh-too fine with Givens. He did not deny what he had done. He lay awake most nights thinking about it in detail and if that was from guilt or simply the fact that he enjoyed gloating over his crimes in the darkness, nobody knew and Givens was not talking. He just wanted to do his time, make no trouble, and get out on the streets again...even though by the state clock that would not be for many, many years, if at all.

"Would you like to pray with me?" Givens said.

"No, I'd rather not," Skiv told him.

Skiv was doing time for molesting several native American boys during his tenure as a reservation student teacher. Givens felt superior to him in that his victims had been female; Skiv, on the other hand, thought he was worlds above Givens because at least his victims were still alive, he had not kidnapped a little girl, brutally molested her, and left her corpse in a shallow grave.

Maybe he'd scarred some little boys for life, but, hey, he hadn't killed anybody.

They were both keeping an eye on the only other person in the room: Palmquist. Funny one. He didn't try to fit in with the other cons nor did he try and hook up with the other losers and rapos. He stayed to himself. When you spoke to him, he barely acknowledged your presence.

Givens had tried to get him to read scripture, but Palmquist wasn't interested in that either.

When a con named Poppy came into the room, both Givens and Skiv visibly tensed. Poppy was just a little guy with bad skin, worse teeth, and graveyard eyes that were constantly searching the yard for new fish to pop. He was the sort of con that went scampering away when guys like Romero, Black Dog, or Riggs came bearing down on him. He did not want to know pain; he only wanted to give it.

Palmquist stared off into space, unconcerned.

Givens and Skiv looked at Poppy quickly, then went back to their respective literature.

Poppy liked that, thought that was funny. As if maybe if they ignored him he would just go away. But he figured they knew better. "Must be rapo central in here," he said. "We got nothing but short-eyed chi-mos as far as the eye can see. I feel like a kid in a candy store." He smiled, revealing his yellowed teeth, giggling with a high repetitive squeaking laugh that was known to go right up spines. "Eeny-meanie-miny-mo, catch a nigger by the toe." He got up close to Skiv, put his hands on the arms of Skiv's chair, leaned in so close Skiv could smell the rank decay of his teeth. "If he hollers, let him go. My mama said to fuck the very best one *and you ain't it!*"

He rasped that last bit right into Skiv's face. Skiv dropped his magazine, badly trembling.

"I said, you ain't *it*," Poppy told him. "Go over to that candy machine. Get a couple Milky Ways, you hear?"

Skiv did but he was trembling so badly he kept dropping the money. He knew what was going on here. This is exactly what had happened to him when he first got to Shaddock Valley. It had happened to Givens more than once. Maybe it was Palmquist's turn.

Thank God, it's not me this time, oh thank God—

Then Tony Gordo came into the room, filling the doorway, picking his teeth with a needle. Gordo was so big he had to stoop over to get in the door and turn himself sideways to fit through it. His head was like a cinder block, a steel gray buzzcut on top and a square jaw below, everything in-between a no-man's land of old knife cuts, cratered scar tissue, and pockmarks sunk so deep you could fit the tip of your thumb into them. He had no neck. That block of a head sat right atop of his shoulders which were nearly as wide as two men standing abreast.

He stood there in his oversized orange jumpsuit, eyes like crouching death taking in his little harem because that was exactly the way he saw things. These were his bitches and he would have them and nobody had better think of stopping him.

As he told Poppy, *Any rapo ass walks through those gates, it belongs to me. I break it, I fuck it, I school it, and I sell it.*

Gordo saw Skiv shivering in the corner and went right over there.

"Please, Mr. Gordo, I—"

Gordo gave him a quick open-hand shot to the face that left a stinging imprint on his brown skin. Skiv was on his knees, sobbing, remembering oh too well what had landed him here and how those boys themselves had sobbed.

"Stand the fuck up, nigger," Gordo told him, his eyes gleaming like dirty nickels. He smiled. There was blood on his teeth from poking his gums with the needle. He did not seem to notice. "Gimme them bars."

Skiv stood up, handed Gordo the candy bars and Gordo very carefully, almost effeminately, unwrapped them. He shoved one after the other into his mouth, working them together into a melting ball of chocolate and caramel. He chewed them slowly, staring at Skiv the entire time, then he swallowed. He grabbed Skiv and pulled him close, running his chocolately tongue over his face. Skiv shook so badly his teeth chattered. A wet, spreading stain appeared at his crotch.

Gordo threw him aside.

He put his eyes on Givens. Givens tried to make a break for it and Poppy took hold of him, held him.

"You're the one that raped that little girl and strangled her," Gordo said. "I enjoyed your sweet ass, oh yes. But it ain't your turn neither. You ladies get out of here."

Poppy giggled.

Givens sobbed.

"Get the fuck out of here," Gordo said. "And close that door behind you. You think of ratting me out and I'll use the both of you every day for a fucking month."

Skiv and Givens raced out the door, slamming it shut behind them.

Gordo turned to Palmquist who stared up at him with dead gray eyes. There was no true fear in those eyes. In fact, there was very little of anything.

Gordo grinned. *This was the one. This was the one Papa Joe wanted to feel some pain. And, good Christ, what a treat that was going to be, hell yes.*

"All right, Palmquist. I been looking for you. Time to go to school. Lights out, motherfucker, lights out for you..."

Palmquist stared at his tormentors. He was not surprised by any of this. He expected it just like he'd expected it at Brickhaven. His eyes were shiny, almost mirrored, just as black as the steaming mud at the bottom of a well. He stared blankly at both men.

"You sure you want this?" he asked them, blinking his eyes.

Poppy started squeaking with laughter. He'd heard a lot of punks say some damned crazy things before Gordo had them, but this beat all and he couldn't stop laughing.

"First thing," Gordo said, "is I like my women to do a little begging so you start getting into the act and I won't hurt you no more than I have to."

"You're making a big mistake," Palmquist told him.

But Gordo didn't see it that way. He moved fast for a big man. Before the words had barely left Palmquist's mouth, he had him in those big grimy fists. He pulled him up into the air and planted a sloppy kiss on his mouth that was all tongue. No romance here, just a beast tasting its food before it took a bite.

And that's when the door opened and Romero came storming in.

"Hey—" Poppy started to say and Romero gave him two quick jabs to the face that opened his nose like a blood blister and brought him to his knees. Romero grabbed him by his greasy hair and kicked him in the stomach. When he folded up he brought his elbow down with considerable force on the back of Poppy's neck and Poppy hit the floor with his eyes rolling.

Gordo tossed Palmquist aside. "Fucking beaner," he said. "You wetback fucking spic fucking bean nigger."

As he moved at Romero, Romero leaped at him, every bit of anger and frustration and deprivation that life behind those walls had inspired in him coming out, boiling out of him like poison. Before Gordo got his hands on him, Romero drilled him in the face with three fast piston-like blows that barely even registered. Then Gordo had him, crushing him in his massive arms. Romero thumbed him in the eye and Gordo responded by delivering a head butt that drove the smaller man right to the floor.

Palmquist, bless him, tried to intervene and Gordo backhanded him, dropping him like a felled tree.

Romero pulled himself up, wiping blood from his face, knowing he was in for pain coming at an animal like Gordo without so much as a shank or a good length of lead pipe in his hands. He ducked as Gordo tried to hit him and got two more good shots in, then kneed Gordo in the jewels. Gordo grunted like a grizzly bear that had been stropped with a belt, but no more.

He hit Romero, piledriving him to the floor.

And before Romero could do more than wonder what day it was, Gordo picked him up and threw him eight feet through the air until he collided with the wall. When he again opened his eyes, there were half a dozen hacks in the room beating Gordo down with their sticks. As he was hauled away for his mandatory thirty days in the hole, Sergeant Warres helped Romero to his feet.

"That big piece of shit started it," Palmquist said.

"Of course, he did, son. He always does." Warres held onto Romero until he could stand on his own. "That's gotta be the most selfless act of suicide I ever did hear of, Romero. Sure as shit. Well, let's get you to the infirmary, get you cleaned up."

As Romero was led away, cons pushing up to the rec room door to see what was going on, he was wondering if he had just punched his own ticket with Papa Joe or if something darker was about to punch Gordo's.

13

Night.

Administrative Segregation.

Jorgensen pulled the duty because Houle was out on sick leave. Kid hadn't been any good since he found what was left of Reggie Weems. Still…sixteen years and here Jorgensen was, pulling the graveyard shift down in the bleak, dripping cellars of Shaddock Valley. He wasn't too happy about it. They had thirty Ad-Seg cells and eight of them were filled now that Tony Gordo was down there. In Jorgensen's way of thinking, Warden Linnard should have kept Gordo down there permanently. He was a fucking animal and he rated a cage.

Rated more than that, I had my way, Jorgensen thought.

He sat at his little desk, a paperback western forgotten on his lap, staring down the corridor at the steel doors which sealed all the bad boys into their private, darkened hells.

All was quiet.

Some nights the shitheads started acting up. One of them started hollering and, just like monkeys in the zoo, the rest started kicking their heels up. Jorgensen wasn't in a good mood. If one of them started, it was going to be a real sorry day in their sorry little books.

He put his feet up, closed his eyes.

He knew he wouldn't sleep because it was damp and chill down there. It had a way of getting under your skin. When he was younger and pulled Ad-Seg, he used to do sit-ups just to keep warm. Maybe he couldn't do so many sit-ups anymore, but he was still hard and stocky. Sixteen years of working society's trash will do that to you.

He started thinking about goddamn Houle and getting angry...but then that led to Reggie Weems and he started feeling the chill dampness down there more than anything else. Weems. And in a locked cell yet. Just like that madness over at Brickhaven—

Hell was that?

He heard a thumping sound from one of the cells down the way, only the more he thought about it the more it registered in his brain as kind of a wet slapping sort of noise. Expecting trouble, he walked down there, feeling his dander rising, and a slow, rising approximation of something quite akin to fear.

The corridor was silent.

The cells were silent.

Not a noise anywhere.

Probably the pipes. They got to making funny sounds down here in the bowels of Shaddock, the steam making them contract, pop and snap. He paused before each cell and listened. Quiet. So quiet in there. Even through the iron doors he could hear a few men snoring. That was good. That was fine. Let it stay like that all night.

But he was not reassured.

Something wasn't right here and sixteen years as a corrections officer had given him a real powerful gut-sense of what was good and what was bad and what was certainly not right. He stopped in front of Gordo's cell, Number #3, even though he'd already paused and listened. It was quiet but he had a very uncanny sort of feeling that someone was standing on the other side of the door, holding their breath, doing everything they could so as not to be heard.

Crazy, you're thinking crazy.

No...there was something.

He pressed his ear to the door and heard a faint rustling followed by what sounded like a dripping. Like water was falling from the ceiling in there.

A thumping noise. Then again.

More rustling, the slap of something like a bare foot on the concrete floor, a moist gurgling sound like Gordo had just worked something snotty and phlegmy from his throat.

The noises could have been explained by a lot of things, but to Jorgensen they were just plain unnatural. That approximation of fear was no longer approximate: it was *real*. It was a dark river, a rising tide and he felt it overtaking him, crawling up his spine and prickling his scalp, settling into his belly with a fluttering volume.

Scraping sounds now...like nails scratched over the walls or maybe claws.

Now a stealthy shifting as of sheets.

Jorgensen knew he was losing it. Sixteen years of this shit and now he was unraveling. He was losing his mind just like they always said it happened to the cons in solitary confinement. But not the guards, never the guards...

He reached up for the bolt that would open the security port, but his hand just wouldn't obey as something in there started thrashing and he heard a weird, unearthly wailing that cut right through him.

And in the seamless, enshrouding blackness of his cell, Gordo began to scream in a high, tormented voice: *"YAHHHH! HELP ME! HELP ME! GET IT OFFA ME! SOMEBODY GET IT THE FUCK OFFA ME—"*

Jorgensen stumbled back and fell right on his ass. The fear was white-hot and ungainly knotted in his belly, spreading out and coiling around his chest in thick bands. He could scarcely draw a breath. It was irrational and suffocating. Around him, the corridor was close and cloistral. He could feel the walls, the darkness that webbed him to the floor.

There was nothing silent in #3 now.

In fact, it sounded like open warfare was raging in there, but Jorgensen knew it was more along the lines of a slaughter. He sat there on his ass as the other cons started shouting and crying out from their cells. Never had he felt more helpless or hopeless. He was shaking, his heart racing, his bladder feeling like an especially juicy melon that was about to blow.

Inside #3, he could hear Gordo screaming, screaming maybe the way his many victims had screamed, but certainly worse...oh yes, certainly worse. But those screams were losing intensity as whatever was in there with him—Jesus, it sounded like the cell was filled with snakes, slithering snakes, brushing the walls and coiling on the floor with smooth sliding sounds— made short work of Tony Gordo, the terror of the streets and wriggling parasite #1 at Shaddock Valley. Whatever it was, it made a wailing/shrieking sort of sound that was pure animal rage somehow coupled with dire human insanity and delivered as an almost hypersonic squealing.

Jorgensen seemed to remember that he was, in fact, a corrections officer. He fumbled for his walkie-talkie. Dropped it, picked it up, dropped it again. When he got it in his hands, his fingers were trembling and clumsy and he could not seem to thumb the button to bring up the channel.

And it was at this time that something started slamming into the iron door with the force of a runaway train, making it tremble in its frame. Whatever it was, it hit it again and again, each time putting dents in it, an iron door two inches thick.

Boom, boom, boom. It kept coming again and again like artillery shells hitting it from the other side, the dents getting larger and what was striking it sounding moister and juicier until mortar began to fall from the walls and concrete dust rose up in a cloud and blood that was bright and shockingly scarlet oozed beneath the door.

And by then, Jorgensen was on his feet, running, shouting into his box with a high, girlish sort of treble that was the sound of the human mind stripped clean by absolute primal terror.

14

After Warden Linnard heard what happened and viewed Ad-Seg cell #3 personally, describing it to his wife as looking like "*someone had opened Gordo up, fingerpainted the walls with what was inside,*" he tried to put a cap on it so the rest of his shitheads didn't hear about it. But in a maximum-security prison with its extremely active grapevine, it was near on impossible. So, deciding he did not make a very effective little boy trying to plug the dike with his finger, Linnard went back to his office and drank half a bottle of Jack Daniels before he got on the phone with the DOC and got his asshole expanded three sizes.

Just as he thought, it was everywhere by noon the next day.

"You heard about Gordo, of course," Aquintez said to Romero out in the yard, knowing that everybody behind those walls had.

"Who hasn't?"

Still aching from his dust-up with Gordo, Romero was scanning the yard, trying to see where it was coming from, trying to spot the meat-hungry eyes zeroing in on him so he'd know which group was going to come after him. Thing was, he saw nothing. The ABs and bikers paid him no mind. The Latin

50

gangs clustered together by the wall, ignoring him. The blacks were gathered together in little groups, involved in their own thing.

Ain't that something, he thought. *I'm warned by Black Dog to lay low and I piss all over that warning. Papa Joe should have psychopaths of every stripe closing in on me...but I don't see any indication of it.*

But it was more than that. You survived long enough in max, you didn't trust your eyes so much as your guts. You got a feeling when danger was coming. It went right up your backbone...but for Romero, today of all days, it just wasn't there.

"Now ain't that something?" he said out loud, not even aware of the fact.

"What you saying, home?"

So Romero told him what he was thinking, how he should have had lots of bad boys putting him in their sights but he wasn't feeling anything and seeing even less.

"They got other things to worry about, home. First Weems and now Gordo...these boys ain't real smart, but even they're making the connection between Palmquist and a real ugly death. He's giving all these lifers and hardtimers bad dreams."

Romero knew that what was in the kid—and he was no longer believing he had imagined any of *that*—had been active again last night. But he hadn't witnessed it because he'd spent the night racked out in the infirmary on sedatives after the doc stitched his face closed from the beating Gordo gave him. So no bad dreams or worse reality for him. But it had happened. He knew that. The kid had fallen asleep and then...

Aquintez told him that he had his ears open and he wasn't hearing anything about Papa Joe putting money out on a certain con named Romero that wasn't playing by the rules.

"Not yet."

"Like I said, people got other things to worry about right now. Besides, home, you're a living legend in this joint. Going after Tony fucking Gordo open-handed without so much as a shank. Now that takes balls, primo balls."

"Or maybe just a lack of common sense, JoJo," Romero said, fingering the bruises and bandages on his face.

Tony Gordo was a walking piece of shit and he got flushed, that's all there's to it.

He felt no pity for the man. He was a crawling worm somebody should have stepped on long ago and who does it? *Palmquist.* Or something inside him. Christ, it was all so buggy, headcase stuff.

He looked around the yard again at all the disinterested cons, but the truth was, he wasn't worrying so much about himself but about the fish, about goddamn Palmquist. Worried that the fear would build and some of the boys would act like the animals they were and kill the kid. That's what worried him.

"I don't know what this is about, man, but I think if they just leave the kid alone, they're gonna be okay."

"Right now, my friend," Aquintez said, "it's gonna take some real dumb motherfuckers to make a play for your boy."

15

But prison life was prison life and it didn't take long before the shit started stirring up again, smelling just as bad as any other day. Three days after Gordo died, Palmquist was put to work in the kitchen with Romero and some of the others. He did his bit all right, doing what the cook told him, stirring a cauldron of brown, greasy meat gravy with a wooden spoon that looked like a broomhandle. Cook said to stir and keep stirring it or it would lump up and the cons wouldn't be able to keep it down.

So Palmquist was stirring and two black guys, cellies named Heslip and Burgon, were whipping instant potatoes in a big mixer, laughing about something and Romero could tell by the way they were laughing and the way they were casting sidelong glances at Palmquist, that it wasn't good.

Palmquist was hearing them, just ignoring what they were saying.

Romero dumped an industrial-size can of green beans into a boiler, tuned in on the conversation.

"Shit, bro, ya'll got me wrong here," Heslip said, looking foolish in his white smock and hairnet. "All I say, all I say here is how I see this bitch first, ought to be me gets to grease his backside."

Burgon just shook his head. "You pull that sweet shit on me last time, fool, I never got a taste. No sir, that boy is mine. I'm taking my crack and you gonna step aside. You can watch you want to, but he be mine."

Christ, they were talking about Palmquist.

Romero felt himself steel at the idea of it. Wasn't none of his business, he supposed, but yet after the Gordo thing, he was making it his business. His old man always said he wasn't the smartest one of the lot, but he was smart enough to know two things: Weems had fooled with the kid and Weems was dead. Same for Gordo. Aquintez had said it was going to take some real dumb motherfuckers to make a play for the fish now and here they were in the flesh. Two more stupid cons looking for an open grave. Maybe it was a wild leap of logic to think that something would happen to them if they persisted, but from where Romero was sitting, he didn't think so.

"All right, shit, you run a hard bargain," Heslip said, pouring more powdered potatoes into the vat. "I give you two cartons Marlboro reds you gimme first dibs on that fine white shit."

"Fuck you say, fool? Two, motherfucker? I don't bite on that. I get you an ounce of good smoke, you forget his ass."

"Shit, I know a whiteboy got serious connections, get you a bottle of Jack Daniels and a couple rocks primo shit. Now what your black ass got to say on that?"

"Shit. You throw in them two cartons, you pop that motherfucker three ways to Sunday."

"Ain't gonna pop him, smoke," Heslip said, like the idea was unthinkable to an upstanding guy like him. "Gonna sell his ass."

Jesus, Romero was thinking, they were bidding on the kid like this was Ebay or some shit. And wasn't that the final, dehumanizing statement of life at Shaddock? Right in front of the kid yet. He wasn't nothing but merchandise to them. But that's the way Heslip and Burgon were. They were both doing life and both had absolutely nothing to lose. They made a habit of jumping on fresh meat when it waltzed its sweet ass through the gates. They would jump it and pump it, school it, then sell it to the highest bidder out in the yard. Romero had seen it done before. Had seen them do it to a young black guy named Lester Heroon, degrading him until he slit his wrists in the showers not two months back.

Romero had to wonder, though, whether this was their idea or maybe Papa Joe had sweetened the pot for them.

They kept at it, now abandoning the potatoes and standing on either side of Palmquist.

"Look at this shit," Burgon was saying. "He young and firm, got that blond hair, looking sweet and solid to me. You saying my boy here, he ain't worth those two cartons, fool?"

"Fuck, I say that? Just, shit, I'm squeezed. How about we run my ass some credit, then we both get what we want."

"What kind of credit line you talking, nigger?"

"Same old, same old, tit for the tat and suck shit, you up on that?"

Palmquist stepped away from them. "Fucking homos," he said. "Fucking nigger homos!"

That shut them up, they came on together, thinking how sometimes you had to break a horse before you could ride it proper.

"*Fuck you say, whitebread?*" Heslip wanted to know.

Romero went over there, not sure if he was trying to save the kid's bacon or that of the two black degenerates. He got in-between them and Palmquist. "Fuck you boys doing, man?" he said, letting that acid fill his voice. "Who say you got a claim on his ass? He's my cellie, bitch. You want to talk business, maybe you better come through me."

"Maybe we ain't going to," Burgon said, big and black and bristling.

Romero pulled a razor out of his belt. "Maybe I'll cut your balls off, make your punk here gargle with 'em. What you got to say to that, home?"

They were watching that razor and not saying a thing. They both knew Romero. Both knew he'd cut lots of guys, did it quick and without warning if you got on his wrong side.

Heslip just smiled, showed lots of bad teeth. "It's cool, Romero, it's cool. What's this shit? This meat belong to you? You got dibs on this shit here?"

Romero shrugged. "Maybe I do. And maybe you ought to think about something real hard and real careful before you lay a hand on him."

"Yeah? What's that, smoke?" Burgon said.

"A con name of Weems fucked with this boy. You know Weems, don't you? Big ass-ugly nigger looked like his mama passed him out her ass? Yeah, he played the game and you know what happened to him. Same went for a white trash meat-eater name of Tony Gordo...or you dumb spades forget that already? They say he was opened like a can of fucking beans. And in solitary. You wanna run that risk?"

They both looked at him like he was crazy and maybe he was, but they both backed off, looked a little tense and gray around the mouth. They didn't have much to say after that.

Palmquist didn't say anything either. But something just behind his eyes was watching them real close.

16

Maybe Heslip and Burgon didn't have much sense, but the other cons surely did. As the day progressed into night at Shaddock, the rumors thickened and the paranoia came with it. Maybe it was imagination and maybe it was plain old superstitious fear, but the cons were feeling something in the prison, something that had not been there before. The atmosphere of the place had never been exactly balloons and parades, but now it was worse. Something was in the air, something dire and oppressive as if the guts had been ripped out of not only Weems and Gordo but the prison itself.

Men were afraid, but they could not admit it.

And worse, they didn't know what they were afraid *of*. But in their minds, in the dark spaces and lonely tracts and locked rooms of childhood terrors, they were seeing things. Lurid shapes and white-faced haunters reaching out for them with hooked fingers. Things birthed from closets and beneath beds, things with moldering grins and shoe-button eyes that whispered your name in the dead of night and sucked the breath from your lungs with black, hungering mouths.

And as the night grew dark as tar and the cons huddled in their cells waiting for lights out, they began to see things reaching out for them from the shadows...

17

Romero hadn't said much to the kid all day. Every time he looked at the little bastard, something flipped over in his stomach and grease bubbled up the back of his throat. His heart started to pound and he couldn't seem to catch his breath. There was something about that kid, just as there had been from the moment Jorgensen had brought him in, something repulsive about him. Something that got inside you, twisted blackly in your guts. He offended Romero and Romero found himself badly wanting to squeeze the stuffing out of the little shit, except...he was afraid of what might come leaking out.

The kid kept thanking him about intervening with Gordo, but Romero didn't want to hear about that shit. Last thing he wanted to be thinking about was Tony Gordo and what happened to him. Especially now. It was lockdown and lights out was coming soon. And he was trapped in the cell with the kid.

So he lay on his rack and read his book and tried not to look at him. Which wasn't easy, because the kid kept looking at him. Palmquist was pacing back and forth, rubbing his palms against his prison-issues, hugging himself, shaking his head. Half a

59

dozen times now he'd stop, pitch a glance at Romero, open his mouth like he was going to say something, then just shake his head and go right on pacing.

"Why don't you fucking relax?" Romero finally said. "You're getting under my skin."

Palmquist sat down, then stood up, sat down again. "It's gonna be dark soon," he said.

"No shit?"

But the kid wasn't having it. He studied his hands, thinking things and maybe wanting to say them, but not daring. He was pale as unleavened flour, his eyes like bruises punched into his face. He was jittery and nervous, couldn't seem to sit still for more than a few moments at a stretch.

"That night," he said. "The night Weems got it...did you hear anything?"

Romero dropped his book an inch or two. "Yeah, I heard you snoring."

"Anything else?"

"What else would I hear?"

Palmquist nodded, rubbed his eyes. "I'm tired."

"So go to sleep, do us both a fucking favor."

But he just shook his head. "I don't want to go to sleep. I don't think I ever want to go to sleep."

"Why is that?"

The kid looked at him and his eyes were practically bleeding. "Oh shit...if you only knew..."

And the bad part was, Romero figured he already did.

18

C Block this time.
     About 2:10 A.M. it started.

There was screaming, but not the screaming of one man but the screaming of two and within seconds after it had begun, like an infectious disease, it spread from con to con on C until they were all going out of their minds.

Bobby Parks pulled the duty.

He had at least ten years on the rest of the guards and when it started, he told them to stay at their stations, told them to get Sergeant Warres right goddamn now.

And then he was running, walkie-talkie in hand, calling for them to unlock doors as he made his way down to the end of C. The cons were out of their minds, hollering and yelling and clattering their bars and demanding to be let out. But Parks ignored them, went numb to all they said and did, concentrated on what was happening down at the end, must have been in cell #75 or #76, that general vicinity. He heard those screams that at first sounded like the inmates were being roasted over coals…gradually becoming something that human lungs were not capable of.

#75, all right.

Parks, big and pumped-up and more than a match for any of the trash that prison could throw at him, suddenly felt very small, very vulnerable, very *afraid*. He was thinking about Houle. About Jorgensen cracking up.

Man up, he told himself. *Man up for chrissake. Do your job.*

But those sounds...Jesus, he didn't know what he was hearing.

A high-pitched screeching that was shrill and strident, piercing his eardrums, making his guts become cold, coiling snakes that twisted and mated, slithering up the back of his throat and filling his mouth. He wanted to turn back the other way, get away from that godawful racket that went right through him, made his molars ache and his marrow go to ice. The cons were all reaching out of their cells, demanding protection or sobbing and screaming, more than a few praying in broken voices.

The screeching was weird and echoing, had the tonal quality of buzzsaws tearing into planks. And there was a stink rising up, too, something flyblown and fermented and dirty.

Parks, his throat full of cinders and dry flaking things, got on his walkie-talkie as he neared #75. "It's me," he said dryly, breathlessly. "Open Seventy-Five..."

"*Open it?*" The guy on the other end clearly couldn't believe it.

"Do what I fucking said..."

Inside the cell, that screeching sound nearly drowned out the noise of things being slammed around, thrown against the bars. Wet sounds, ripping sounds, sounds like axes hacking into raw meat. Sounds Parks could not believe...the sound of something moving with moist undulations like snakes sliding out of swamps across wet leaves.

Parks edged in closer, clicked on his flashlight and saw—

He wasn't sure what he saw, only that it made him take two fumbling steps back and that he nearly dropped his flashlight. He saw Heslip...he thought it might be Heslip...come slamming up against the bars and at such an amazing velocity, Parks almost screamed himself. Heslip slammed into the iron rungs like he'd been hit by a truck, propelled with such force you could hear his bones breaking with the impact. A mist of something warm and wet sprayed onto Parks, the lens of his flashlight was hit with clots of tissue that obscured the light, threw big black blobs into the beam.

And in that grim instant, before he was yanked away, Parks saw that Heslip was drenched red like he'd been dipped in red ink and his body...broken and contorted, his face a bleeding husk, entirely fleshless like somebody had carved the meat away with a knife.

Then Heslip was yanked back and away.

Parks' flashlight was jumping in his hand, the light creating leaping night-shapes and it was impossible to say what was happening in there. And although he didn't know it, it had been less than ten seconds since he'd approached #75. But everything was pulled out like taffy, becoming nightmarish and surreal. All those cons raging in their chorus of dementia and Parks hearing slobbering, hungry sounds from inside the cell and the clattering resonation of things like teeth on bones and nails clicking and scraping. Crazy, insane shit. His bobbing flashlight was showing him blood and motion and anger, something slashing around in there, writhing and shrieking. A glistening, whipping helix of gas and flesh and pulsating ropes, pissing steam and gray jelly.

And then Parks heard something that slapped him back into reality: the clicking of the cell lock. The door began to slide back and Parks, crying out with everything he had into the walkie-talkie said, "*Close that fucking door! Close that fucking door you goddamn asshole close it!*"

The door stopped and began shutting.

It had only made it maybe three feet, but it was enough. Enough for something to slink out, a mass of pink translucent tentacles like things that might belong to a jellyfish. They coiled out like blind worms, searching, feeling their way along and then Parks *did* scream. They got within three feet of his left boot and then the door closed on them, trapping them there and finally severing them in a spray of inky fluid that stank like rotting fish. In the cell, that abomination let go with a keening, reverberating squeal like a dozen teakettles whistling simultaneously. The severed tentacles looped obscenely like worms in direct sunlight and Parks dropped his light and screamed into his walkie-talkie for them to turn on the lights, turn on the main fucking lights, and the cons all around him were bellowing out prayers to Jesus and Mother Mary and then those lights came on. Exploded with a brilliance that made Parks squeeze his eyes shut.

And the thing in there began wailing as if it had been doused with acid as the light found it. There was smoke and fog and a mist of blood and that thing shrieking with rage and hatred, then a grinding/groaning sound of metal ripping and bolts snapping off. By the time Parks could get a good look, he saw that whatever it was, was gone. It had peeled the cover off the radiator vent and slipped into the ventilation system.

Sergeant Warres was there by then, wanting to know what in Christ was going on, what the hell had happened this time. But then he saw the slaughterhouse in #75, the bones and meat and blood and he turned away.

"*What the hell was it?*" he put to Parks.

But Parks just shook his head, eyes bulging and drool hanging from his mouth. "It...it was pissed off," he managed.

19

Warden Linnard put Palmquist down in solitary for his own protection. The cons had made the connection between what had happened at Brickhaven and what was happening here and now at Shaddock Valley. And that morning, after the slayings of Heslip and Burgon, about twenty cons half out of their mind with terror jumped the kid in the mess hall and beat him senseless before the guards put the whole thing down. As it was, Palmquist needed thirty stitches and his left arm had to be put in a sling.

"Listen," Linnard told him. "I don't like this shit that's coming down here. These men want to kill you and they will, given the chance, so I'm placing you under protective custody. Not in the PC cells, but down in the hole. It's the most secure environment we have and, pending a state investigation, that's where you're going to stay."

The warden told Palmquist that he didn't know if he was responsible for any of that shit or not and he honestly couldn't see how he could have been, but into the hole he was going. For safekeeping. The warden had trouble like he'd never seen before. The cons were out of their heads and jailhouse lawyers were writing up writs and lawsuits against the Department of

Correction. And the DOC was all over Linnard's ass and the state had ruled that the Shaddock Valley complex was to be off-limits to the press until further notice.

And in the prison, tensions seethed and boiled and slowly came to a head, feeding off long-standing gripes and unanswered complaints about treatment and living conditions. Romero knew what was coming.

They all knew what was coming. Except maybe Linnard. If he had sensed what was about to happen he would have placed the entire prison in lock-down.

The warden chose Romero to bring Palmquist his meals, thought maybe the sight of his cellmate would make the kid feel less like he was being punished and more like he was being given special treatment. Romero didn't want to pull that bit, but he knew if he refused the warden, the warden would get on the hacks and the hacks would get on him.

So he brought Palmquist his supper—greasy green bean casserole and a few wedges of rye bread that were more rye than bread—and the hack let him in, let him sit in there with the kid for a few moments, even shut the door behind him.

Palmquist didn't look so good, what with the contusions and the stitches and the cast on his arm. But it was more than just the beating he took. His face was moon-white and his eyes were ponds of black, simmering liquid sunken into red-rimmed sockets. To Romero, he looked like a guy coming off heroin, like his soul had been milked dry.

He didn't say anything at first, so Romero said, "Tell me about it, Cherry. Tell me all about it."

But the kid did not lift his head. "I...can you get me some speed, Romero? Some Dexedrine or uppers? Caffeine pills even? Anything like that? Something that'll keep me awake. I don't care what it is."

"Probably," Romero told him. "If I can get it past the hog out there."

"If you can't do that, get me a fucking razor."

Romero just watched him. Suicidal now. He had sunken that low. Romero knew, of course, what had happened to Heslip and Burgon. He'd heard all about it that morning. But unlike the affair with Weems, Romero had slept through it...with a little help from some sedatives. "You think that's the answer, Cherry? Pills and razors?"

"I can't go to sleep," Palmquist said in a cool, lifeless voice. "Maybe not ever again, but sure as hell not tonight."

"Why is that?"

"You know why."

Romero figured he did. "I heard it," he said, sighing. "I heard it the night it got Weems. I heard something up there with you and you know what, Cherry? It scared the piss right out of me. I heard that business up in your bunk, but I didn't have the balls to go and look."

"I'm glad you didn't, he..."

"Yes?"

Palmquist just shook his head. "I hated Weems and Gordo, those other two..."

"Nothing but trash, Cherry. Human trash."

"...yeah, sure, but you gotta believe me, Romero, I never meant for them to...oh Jesus, this has gone way too far and I'm to blame. All those cons, they fucking hate me and they want me dead. I wish they'd killed me this morning." He said it and he meant it, too. You could hear the pain in his voice. "Funny, ain't it? All day long I been wishing they'd killed me. It's the only thing that sounds good to me right now."

Romero thought about it long and hard. He lit a cigarette, blew the smoke out through his nostrils. "Tell me something, Cherry. Whatever's going on with you, it's happened before, hasn't it? I mean, c'mon, this...whatever in the fuck it is...it can't be a new thing."

"It's not."

"It targets your enemies, doesn't it?"

"Anything it thinks is a threat to me."

Romero put a hand on his arm, said, "C'mon, kid, what the hell is this about?"

Palmquist chuckled low in his throat, dropped his face into his hands. "You wouldn't believe me. Nobody would. I've told other people...they thought I was nuts."

Romero pulled on his cigarette. "Shit, I'd believe anything by this point, kid. Really, I would." He paused. "Okay. Let me tell you then. It's this brother of yours, dammit. You called him *Damon* that first day. I remember. You said he wasn't like other people, he was different. That if somebody fucked with you...he'd straighten them out. Except, well, I thought he was on the outside, but he's on the inside, isn't he? *He's inside you.*"

"Yes, he is." Palmquist clenched his teeth, scratched fingers over his scalp. "He's always been in me. See, Romero, I was one of a set of twins. My brother, he died at birth. Well, he was already dead. Sometimes, when you have twins in the womb, one of them will assert its dominance and absorb the other one. I was the dominant one, though sometimes I don't think that's true at all..."

Palmquist said sometime in the first trimester of his mother's pregnancy she had an ultrasound, and they discovered twin boys in her womb. She named the boys Danny and Damon. Whichever came out first was to be Danny, the other Damon.

Only Damon never came out at all.

By the second trimester, there was only Danny and some rudimentary tissue that had never taken. It was absorbed by the other fetus. Rare at that date, the doctor told her, but it did happen.

"She told me about it when I was like five or six. My old man died in a car accident and I guess it was time for confessions," Palmquist said. "Part of me already knew, because somehow, someway, I always knew I was never alone. I just *sensed* it, I guess, and as the years passed, that sense of another in me grew stronger and stronger. No, Damon never came out, never really formed, but what he was, it hid inside me."

Palmquist said he never really talked to Damon, was never in direct contact with this other because Damon only had dominance when he was sleeping…then, only then, would he come out. Come out and play. Palmquist would wake up in the morning when he was a kid and his toys would be in disarray, things moved and sometimes things broken or lost entirely. It was Damon. He would come out at night and play like any other child. But he was not like any other child. Palmquist sensed this right away as a kid. Whatever Damon was, it was something that had taken the shape of all the awful, black and grotesque things that hide in the subcellar of children's minds. Things from closets and ditches.

"When kids would pick on me, Damon would get them at night," Palmquist admitted in a low, wounded voice. "Oh, he wouldn't kill them or anything. Maybe pinch them or bite them or push them out of bed. By the time I was a teenager, he got more vicious, more aggressive, you know? All those hormones must have touched him, too, and when some kids picked on me, Damon would pay them back. A girl made fun of me endlessly in ninth grade Bio. Called me a faggot and all that. Damon twisted the head off her dog. He pushed another kid down a set of stairs, clawed the shit out of a bully that was tormenting me. Candy Boggs. She was a popular chick, a real looker. I got up the balls and asked her out. She laughed in my face and she and her friends taunted me for days. Damon visited her one night. I don't know what he did to her, but she ended up in a psycho ward for almost a year..."

Insane as it all was, Romero could see it happening, that hideous brother hiding inside, coming out to protect the only thing in the world he really loved. If such a thing *could* love. "That girl...the one he killed and got you here—"

"That was the first time he murdered anyone," Palmquist said with complete honesty. "I swear to God, it was. Then came Brickhaven...and, well, I suppose you know the rest. He's part of me just as I'm part of him. I'd wish him away if I could, you know? But it's not that simple."

The guard opened the slot in the door. "All right, Romero, you two can suck tongue another time."

The slot closed.

As Romero made to rise, Palmquist put a hand on his arm. "Those guys who did this to me...Damon will hunt them down one by one. Do you understand, Romero? Keep away from them. Especially at night." Palmquist released his arm. "He's afraid of the light. Remember that, okay? And tell the hacks to leave the lights on in here or things are going to happen."

Romero nodded. "Tell me something, kid. We're okay, you and me...right?"

Palmquist managed a smile. "Of course we are. You're a good guy, Romero. I knew the moment I saw you that you wouldn't let anything happen to me. Not if you could help it."

"Maybe you know me better than I know myself."

"And that thing with Gordo...man, that was really something."

Romero just shrugged.

"You made us feel safe," Palmquist told him. "I know you've been through the system and had it tough all the way...but you're one of the good ones. You really made us feel safe, feel protected..."

And then the hack opened the door and dragged Romero out and Romero felt a lump of something in his throat, quickly swallowing it down as he remembered who he was and where he was and that this was no place for such things.

"Keep the light on in there," he told the guard.

But the hack just laughed. "Your boyfriend afraid of the dark, Romero?"

"No, but after tonight, I bet *you* are."

20

At Shaddock Valley, they weren't many people Romero trusted.

Surely, not the hacks and precious few prisoners. But JoJo Aquintez was one of them. The state had dropped him for eight years on an armed robbery conviction. He was a tough boy and his little vacation at Shaddock was the second time the state had sent him away to college. But for all that and for all the swindling and menacing he'd done in his time, Aquintez was all right in Romero's way of thinking. He was a good guy to have at your side. When you were his friend, you could trust him absolutely. He wouldn't steal from you, snitch on you, or try to ram a homemade knife into your back.

And in a maximum-security prison, that was saying something.

Romero was being up front about what he knew, exhuming all the demented little secrets from the black soil of his soul, rattling yellowing skeletons from closets he would just as soon have left bolted. "I know it's fucking jiggy crazy stuff, JoJo, but I swear to it on my mother's grave. Palmquist...Jesus...he ain't like other people. That shit he was saying about his brother, well, it's true."

"I believe it. I think we all believe a lot of things we didn't believe before, don't we?" Aquintez said quietly as was his way. "Things have a way of adding up. Even things we'd rather not let ourselves believe."

Aquintez was about 5'6 with shoes on, but stocky and powerful from working the iron pile in the gym. He wore glasses, slicked his thinning hair straight back from his high forehead, and was into Medieval history of all things. He had read every book in the prison library on the subject and had read about a hundred more through inter-library loans and purchases.

He wasn't your average con.

But then, as Romero had learned in his many wasted years in lock-ups and hard-time state joints, there was no such thing as your average con. Some were jailhouse lawyers and some were artists, others were poets and still others were farmers at heart. And many others, of course, were just plain hoodlums and bullies and homicidal maniacs. One thing you could never put in a box were cons...figuratively, anyway.

"I gotta tell somebody this shit," Romero said, "so it might as well be you."

"I'm listening."

"Palmquist...you see...he had this twin..."

Aquintez smoked a cigarette and listened, patiently, absorbing every word and weighing them out carefully in his mind. And it was a good mind. One that easily picked out implications, subtle nuances, and unspoken possibilities. So he smoked and listened and watched the cons out in the yard playing their games, strutting around like randy males with no females to impress.

"He's really a good kid, JoJo," Romero finished by saying, his face sweaty and his eyes blinking rapidly as if he were trying to blink away some image he couldn't bear to look upon. "We could have made him into a good con, one that knew the ropes but wasn't like those guys out there. I really believe that. What happened to Weems and Gordo and Heslip and Burgon—"

"Those pricks deserved what they got and we both know it," Aquintez said, just stating a fact that was widely known.

Romero nodded. "I guess what I'm saying is that we can't blame the kid for any of that, he's not really responsible for...for his brother."

"Of course not. Man, the tales people have been telling around here—about the kid having a demon guardian and shit, about him being some kind of antichrist, having psychic powers like those little blonde bastards in that English movie there— well, what you're telling me now ain't any harder to swallow." He shrugged. "In fact, it's a lot easier. As far out and implausible as it might seem, at least we have something of a scientific explanation...shit, straight out of the *Outer Limits*, but it's at least something we can get our hands on."

"Don't make me feel much better," Romero said.

Aquintez smiled thinly. "At least it's not ghosts and demons here. You'll never get those dumb shits out there to believe it, but I do. Let me get this straight," he said, crushing out his cigarette. "The kid's twin...Damon, you say? When the kid is asleep, this twin that somehow never died but crawled deep inside him can externalize himself physically?"

"Yeah."

"Fucking unbelievable."

"Scares the shit out of me," Romero admitted, not ashamed to do so. "If you had heard it..."

"What...what *did* you hear?"

"Oh, it was crazy, I thought I was going to scream," Romero said in a high, squeaking voice. "I was laying there and I heard movement. I smelled something like rotten fruit but bad enough to gag you. And those sounds...it must have been

74

pulling itself out of the kid, coming out of his head and I heard it, *I fucking heard it*...like somebody was pulling the guts out of a pig. And that stink, the sounds it made sliding along the wall, oh Jesus and Mary..."

"But you only heard it the night Weems was put down?"

"The night it got Gordo I was in the infirmary and when it got Heslip and Burgon, I took enough Seconal to drop a bull elephant. I slept right through it. I knew what was going to happen and I just couldn't bear to *hear* it..." Romero clutched his hands together to stop them from shaking. "Something has to be done, JoJo, but I just don't know what."

Aquintez shook his head. "Nothing we can do but stay on that kid's good side. You know what's coming here, I think we all do..."

Romero did.

And if it came down, well the kid wouldn't survive it. Because they were talking riot here. It had been whispered about for years, but now it looked like it might happen. The four brutal murders at the prison had acted as sort of a catalyst and now everyone was talking it, black and white and Hispanic. For once they were all together on something.

And when it came down, not *if*, the cons would take over the place. One of the first things they'd do after taking control of Shaddock, as all cons did in a riot, would be to storm the PC units where the snitches and weaklings were kept. Then they'd liberate prisoners from Ad-Seg.

And Danny Palmquist? They'd kill him on sight.

21

I f ever there was a prison that was inviting an uprising, it was Shaddock Valley.

It was an ancient place dating from the early 19th century and precious few improvements had been made in all that time. It was cold as a mountain ice house in the winter and hot enough to make paint run in the summer. A drafty, leaking, bug-infested hellhole that was old by the time of the First World War and positively decrepit as the millennium approached and then passed. As Shaddock limped into its third century of existence, it remained what it had always been: a dump where the state stowed away its garbage and then turned a blind eye when the rats and maggots started coming out.

Prisoners complained about everything from the food to sanitation to accommodations and were answered by stony silence. Same went for improved medical care and visitation rights, simple things like better mattresses and access to a dentist once every third year.

The guards were vicious and beatings were commonplace...as were weeks spent in the hole over minor and often manufactured offenses. The white boys had it hard and the blacks and Hispanics just a little bit harder. The guards were corrupt and would smuggle in anything from bone movies to drugs if you paid them to do so. But what cost a white man $20, cost a Latino $30, and a black $50. The guards encouraged snitches, even paid inmates to rat on each other...which they did with unsettling regularity. The guards also believed in divide and conquer. Sometimes, out of the blue, they gave certain black prisoners privileges, while denying them to whites, thereby increasing race hatred and encouraging violence which always came sooner or later, usually in the form of blacks and whites going at each other out in the yard with sawed-off pipes and shanks. Sometimes the guards gave special treatment only to certain individuals within a racial group, then made bets on how long it would be before his friends threw him a beating...or worse.

The guards spread rumors, routinely told prisoners lies about their wives and family, anything to stir the pot and make their rodents run the maze. On any given day, inmates could expect their cells to be tossed. Personal belongings were confiscated, drawings made by their children ripped up, pictures of girlfriends taken away and sold to other inmates...and particularly if said girlfriend was wearing a bathing suit or a sexy outfit.

The guards were, for the most part, country boys.

Big, brutal rednecks who hated anyone darker than white on sight. The blacks were beaten on a regular basis and the Hispanics just barely tolerated...unless their English wasn't real good, then they were officially made prime targets. White criminals such as organized crime types were fawned over and idolized by the guards who waited on them hand and foot, bringing in food from Italian delis for them, wine, fresh fruit and select cuts of meat. Black organized crime figures of no less stature could expect to be thrown in the hole or beaten if it looked like they might try to unify the loose collection of black gangs into a single entity.

Jailhouse lawyers were also hated by the guards.

Starvation rations were commonplace for so much as hinting at filing a writ. Country music was tolerated, but rap and hard rock would get your radio or boombox confiscated and particularly if the guards fancied having it for their own. Letters from home were stalled if you were considered a troublemaker and any outgoing mail was read before being posted. And any tidbits of a personal or intimate nature they could glean from your mail were used to harass you with.

Such was life at Shaddock Valley.

The DOC liked to talk prison reform, but it was yet to be seen at Shaddock. And like old sores that have never been properly treated, only allowed to scab over, the bile and poison built up until it contaminated every nerve ending and strand of muscle, made the blood run toxic, and the entire diseased body of the prison was filled with infection.

And it was only a matter of time before somebody lanced it.

22

It was a bad night.

There were never any truly good nights at Shaddock when you didn't have a prisoner going after another or vomiting in his cell or throwing piss at a passing guard, but some were just plain worse than others. And some guards just seemed to pull the worse duty night after night.

Leo Comiskey was like that.

He seemed to be on permanent duty down in the hole, watching the Ad-Seg prisoners, hearing their endless gripes and complaints, listening to them scream in the dark and beg for the lights to be turned on. Even through those iron doors, you could hear them...but muffled and tinny like a voice coming from a buried box, filtered by soil.

There were seven guys in Ad-Seg at present and they were all nervous and scared to a man. And the reason for this was that an eighth prisoner had been added: Danny Palmquist. The way they were acting, you would have thought he was maybe the Devil or something that had oozed into the joint to suck their blood and lick their brains out of their skulls. Because there was no getting around one thing: they were frightened, terrified even. And these were big boys, tough boys, the kind of

79

boys you didn't dare turn your back on unless you wanted a razor across your throat.

Comiskey didn't care for it.

Because he knew what was going on with Palmquist and it wasn't just the cons that were afraid of him. The guards, even the warden...they all got a funny look about them when the kid's name was mentioned, like maybe they needed to get sick and couldn't find a good place.

And what surely wasn't helping anything was the yellow crime scene tape over the door to cell #3 where Tony Gordo had died. No, that didn't help at all.

Two of the cons down there were newbies, both had swallowed drugs (it was suspected) and both were on shit watch. And that was a real treat for any guard, having to check a con's stools. Jesus.

It was midnight when the sounds started coming from Palmquist's cell. Funny, high-pitched squealing noises that went right up Comiskey's spine and echoed around in the back of his head like screams heard in the dead of night.

Comiskey called it in, went over to the door to #14 where the kid was.

He reached up for the bolt that would open the little security port. But like Jorgensen days before, that's about as far as his hand got...because something inside him literally pulled his hand back. Like a man taking a swan dive off a ten-story building, it wanted him to think very carefully about what it was he was doing.

So Comiskey stood there, shivering like something yanked from a deep-freeze, remembering with an almost vibrant clarity the stories the other guards were telling about what they'd heard and—in the case of a few unlucky correctional officers—had actually *seen*.

There are some things in life, Sergeant Warres had told his guards in an ominous whisper, *that you get in your craw and they don't never leave you. Things that'll turn your hair fucking white and make you sleep with the lights on. You boys seen what I saw, you get a look at it and had that smell rubbed in your face, you got all you can do not to stick your service pistol in your mouth...*

And there was truth to that, Comiskey got to thinking. Maybe Warres was a bossy, brutal asshole, but that didn't mean he was wrong. All you had to do was ask Jorgensen...except he'd had a nervous breakdown and wouldn't be doing any talking for some time to come.

These were the things bouncing around in Comiskey's head like stray bullets, chewing up everything in their path. He was hearing that shrill, mournful wailing like the kid had given birth to something seeded in hell, and his fingers were on that bolt, shaking, cold, colder than cold. So goddamned cold he could barely feel them.

Do it for chrissake, he told himself, *just do it.*

He threw the bolt and a blast of air came out at him, hot and yeasty and offensive and his guts tried to crawl out his ass or up his throat. And that stink, worse by the second, boiling and sulfurous, hitting him full in the face like tear gas, making his eyes water and his throat constrict and his nostrils burn.

He clicked on the light.

Palmquist was lying on the bed, dead asleep maybe, and he was covered in a net of white, cobwebby material like ectoplasm. It was coming out of his mouth and ears and eyes and trailing from his fingertips in ropy, pulsing tendrils that seemed to be alive. The netting was undulating as if it were breathing, trailing up to the ceiling and there, right there, connected to that stuff and splayed out was something pale and bloated and spider-like—

Jesus.

It was getting larger, swelling up like rising bread dough.

That's what Comiskey saw.

He saw it for maybe a second, no more than two, and then the thing shrieked and hissed and scrambled over the ceiling, tangled up in that white goo that looked oddly like silly string.

Comiskey screamed and shut the port.

Behind the door, that grotesque horror squealed and roared and whined like metal on a grinding wheel. Then...slowly, slowly, it began to subside. There were awful sounds coming from inside the cell. Things like cement poured into buckets, wet laundry slapped against the walls, someone pissing on the floor. Then Palmquist began to moan and then...nothing.

After that, Comiskey left the light on.

23

The riot began the next morning.

The blacks started it. Fed up with conditions and mistreatment and bullshit promises from lawyers, they seized the moment and took over the yard, disarming about twenty hacks and dousing them with hidden cans of kerosene, holding matches in their hands and calling out to the machine gunners and snipers in the towers to back off or they'd torch them.

That's all it took.

The hacks didn't like it, but they weren't about to see their brother hacks toasted like wienies, so they withdrew. First thing they did after slipping back was to get on the bullhorns and promise the prisoners that the payback for this one was going to be of biblical fucking proportions.

Just as the blacks were the catalyst in the yard, the whites and Hispanics were the catalysts just about everywhere else. They grabbed maintenance workers and administrative personnel and hacks on break, took over the armory and the warden's office and pretty soon, the fight was over before it had even begun.

Shaddock Valley belonged to the inmates.

Romero was in the metal shop when it started. He could feel it in the air, tensions rising like a barometer before a hot, violent storm. Every con knew what was happening. Every con felt it, every con understood the body politic of what was coming next. By the time Romero got his head full of that stink which was the smell of freedom, baby, and the labor pains it would take to bring it to term, the three hacks in the metal shop had been beaten to the floor and the siege began.

One of them, a big hairy fellow named Knapp who looked like maybe he spent his free hours in bearskins hunting mastodon, spit out a mouthful of blood and said, "Fucking animals, you fucking animals, your time's coming and when it does, they'll kill every one of your baby-raping asses—"

But that's all he got out because a wiry black guy called Skinner cracked him in the mouth with the business end of a lead pipe and Knapp the ape-man gagged out most of his teeth. He was in pain, godawful pain, but still you couldn't get that hate out of his eyes, that leering demented hatred for the men brutalizing him. So Skinner split his head open with the pipe and a biker named Skaggs shoved him aside, and slit Knapp's throat with a straight razor.

Blood.

It was running out in the yard and administration buildings, rec rooms and prison industries...pools and creeks and glistening iron rivers...but for the boys in the metal shop this was their first real taste of a hack's blood, his death-blood and its smell was raw and meaty and metallic. They all started hollering and hooting like a pack of slat-thin dogs drooling over a joint of beef. They rushed in and kicked and stomped and pounded Knapp until he was broken and mangled, pissing red like a water balloon full of crushed cherries. His head looked very much like a ripe tomato, its juice leaking everywhere.

The cons saw that, too, of course.

They saw how spoiler's bled, how hacks went prostrate and shattered to their gods just like anyone else. Just like they all would when the governor lost his cool and told the cops, *take those fucking animals down, crush 'em like goddamn insects and shovel what's left into the trash. Any still crawling when it's done, kick 'em into their cages and lock 'em down, dirty murdering animals, the day of reckoning is at hand for their filthy asses…*

So the cons stood around the wreckage of Knapp while the other hacks moaned and swore and called their mothers whores. They stood there, eyes bright and feral, tongues wetting lips and hands clenched tightly on pipes and wrenches and shards of metal wrapped in duct tape.

Romero had seen mob ugliness before.

He knew its smell, its taste, the way it got down inside your belly and unwound the coils of your guts with cold fingers. But this…this just wasn't acceptable. If they were going to show the DOC and the media that they were just human beings scratching for decent treatment and not blood-hungry savages, then this was not how it was done.

"You can't do it like this, you fucking morons!" he cried out at them. "Don't you see? Don't any of you see? This is exactly what they expect and it's what they want. You're playing into their hands…"

But the cons didn't seem to see at all.

They were all staring at Romero, eyes shining with steel-hard mob mentality. It seeped from them like poison.

These were bad boys. Here were your white supremacists and Black Muslims, Hispanic triggermen and redneck sociopaths. Race had ceased to exist and the dawn-call of savagery was their inheritance. Hell's Angels and ABs, Vice Lords and Gangster Disciples, Spanish Cobras and Nuestra Familia, all standing shoulder to shoulder, breathing in each other's hate and exhaling a communal atavism. Their teeth were

85

bared, spit hung from their lips, their fists were white-knuckled on weapons and in their bellies was the rumble of blood-hunger and death-hunger. Romero took a step back because, God help him, he thought they were going to drop on him in a pack. Stun him like a cow in a Chicago stockyard, hoist him up by his ankles and yank his goodies out, go charging down the corridors in an ensanguined posse, his severed head held high on a pole.

But it didn't happen.

Skaggs stepped forward, Skinner at his side. The chief and the tribal medicine man, both splattered with blood and bits of tissue.

"You wanna stay alive, you fucking mite," Skaggs said in a voice just as rough as scraping gravel, "then you better shut the fuck up. You better decide if you're with us or with them, because if you ain't with us…"

"Like he say," Skinner piped in. "You ain't with us…ha, ha, your death gonna be one scary motherfucker."

Romero held his hands out. It was an ancient gesture, showing you carried no weapons. Worked good with rabid dogs and men who weren't much above them on the evolutionary scale. "All I'm saying is that this is what those cocksuckers expect of us. They expect us to kill hacks and rape the weaklings, burn and loot and pillage…we gotta show 'em that we're above that, that we just want decent treatment."

"You don't know cock," Skaggs said and pushed past him.

The others fell in step, brushing past Romero and staining him with blood as they passed. When they hit the outside air, they all started running. Running and shouting and looking for something or someone to bring down.

Romero sighed, looked over at the two hacks who were still alive, beaten severely, but alive. They were tied to lathes. This was the point in some shitass Hollywood flick, he knew, where the lone convict helps the hacks that would never help him.

Yeah, right.

"Just keep your fucking mouths shut," he told them. "And maybe they'll forget about you. It's the best you can hope for."

Then he turned and went to see a riot firsthand. Figured he better get a good look before the police and army brought them all down and smashed them to cider like apples rotting under trees.

24

The riot.

It was quite a picture.

Cons roaming in gangs and posses with knives and pipes and razors, guns from the armory. The whites out in force along with the blacks and Hispanics. Everyone on a rampage. Three guards were dead within the first hour as long-simmering hatreds boiled over and the men found weapons in their hands. The offices were demolished. The prison industry buildings set on fire. The Ad-Seg and protective custody cells were opened and all the rats and weaklings and celebrity inmates were torn to pieces by roving mobs.

Romero made it out into the yard and it was chaos.

Utter chaos.

Helicopters were in the air and the state police were assembling outside the walls with SWAT units and tear gas and sharpshooters. The National Guard had been mobilized. The authorities were calling out over loudspeakers for the cons to surrender, for the hostages to be released. A bunch of outlaw bikers tossed the corpse of a guard over the wall in response.

But through it all, there was a loose sort of unity amongst the convicts themselves. The whites were led by Mafia soldiers and bolstered by the ABs, biker gangs, and hundreds of renegade criminals just itching for a fight. The blacks were led by a cocaine trafficker doing life who had managed to cement together all the street gangs and drug dealers and pimps. The Hispanics were led by a high-ranking member of the Mexican Mafia. Out in the yard, the whites assembled along one wall, the blacks another, and the Hispanics yet another.

But in the center, with the hostages, there were some of each.

By nightfall, these three leaders had calmed the mobs and began making demands over the loudspeakers. At first, they were ignored, but when they announced they'd kill one person for each hour if their demands were not met, they were flooded with responses.

The negotiating went on well into the night.

The prison was swept by searchlights, cordoned off by police and National Guard units. The news media was out in force, but the cops wouldn't let them within a mile of Shaddock.

Around midnight, the authorities broke off negotiations.

Then they turned off the water.

Then the lights.

25

Romero was on the far side of the yard, watching the bonfires and the smoke billowing up into the night sky from burning buildings. The cons were still agitated, but many were drunk and stoned, laughing and cheering and talking freedom and brotherly love. Romero had been listening to speeches and crazy schemes all day. But unlike many of the others, he wasn't naïve enough to believe any of it.

Sooner or later, this was going to meltdown and the body count would be high. Either the cons would go after each other or the cops would storm the place and take care of business.

It could come from any direction, but Romero was only concerned about Palmquist.

"I found him," Aquintez said, out of breath from running across the yard and wherever it was he'd come from. He pulled Romero away from a group of cons smoking a joint. "I found the kid."

"Where?"

Aquintez told him. Down in the hole. The cons had piped him, cracked his head good. He was out cold and they couldn't revive him. They brought him up to the infirmary.

"He's in a bad way, man," Aquintez said. "If he ain't dead, he's gonna be soon. In a coma or something. You gotta see that infirmary. Fucking bodies everywhere. Some blacks are running the place, they got a couple hacks tending to the wounded."

Romero sighed. The kid was still alive then. Was that a good thing or a bad thing? He tossed his cigarette. "This could be real bad, JoJo. That thing in him...his brother...it's already pissed off about the beating the kid got and now this."

"And it's dark out," Aquintez said. "Pitch fucking black."

A chill went up Romero's spine. "I'm going up there."

Aquintez said that wasn't a good idea. As he passed through the yard on the way to the administration building where the infirmary was, he could hear the cops out there. It sounded like maybe they were scaling the walls, positioning themselves.

"I'm going anyway."

Aquintez clapped him on the shoulder. "Ah, Romero, the original Latino James Cagney. Heart too big and balls twice that size. Okay, I go with you, my friend."

But what they were going into, they had no idea.

26

It started right away.

With sirens shrilling and hostage negotiators working the loudspeakers, nobody realized it until it was too late. The SWAT teams were beginning the engagement, the spearhead of a larger force that would crush anything that stood in its way. By the time Romero and Aquintez got around the chapel, got a look at the administration building, they saw black forms running along the tops of the wall like scurrying spiders and the tear gas started dropping. Canisters were fired into the air, exploding on impact. There were bright flashes and popping, hollow explosions like the compound was under mortar attack. The gas detonated with rolling, noxious clouds. Not just outside the administration building, but in the yard, on rooftops and walkways, just about everywhere.

And more canisters were dropping by the moment.

You could hear cons screaming and firing weapons, the reports of sniper rifles taking out prisoners at strategic points and the answering volleys of small arms fire from the convicts themselves. But in the darkness with only bonfires to see by and most of the cons drunk and stoned and confused, it was a turkey shoot. The SWAT teams had night-vision goggles and the cons had stick matches, some flashlights, and a variety of crude torches. Water cannons were hoisted atop the walls at the same time the snipers fired their first shots, many from silenced weapons. Before the enraged cons could even think of setting the hacks on fire, gouts of water hosed them down, wetting the hacks and knocking their abductors flat with high-pressure streams. Then tear gas. Stun grenades.

The troops moved in for the deathblow.

By that time, Romero and Aquintez had made the administration building, coughing and gagging and rubbing their eyes, steering themselves through the maze of corridors and climbing sets of steps with nothing more to see by than a penlight and the strobing flashes from outside.

"They're tearing 'em up out there," Aquintez said, panting.

And they were. The cons were screaming and shouting, begging for mercy. And the police were answering this with salvos of plastic bullets fired from automatic weapons and light machine guns.

But the screaming wasn't only outside.

It was above, too: on the fourth floor where the infirmary was.

Romero and Aquintez looked at each other in the churning darkness, the smell of death and teargas blowing in from outside and combining into a vile aroma with what was coming down from the fourth-floor stairwell: a rancid, hot stench of blood and misery.

They started up.

They vaulted up the steps, hearing sounds and smelling things and feeling something like sheaths of needles unfolding in their bellies. In the corridor at the top, they could hear a wild, spiraling voice shattering like glass: "*Help me! Help me! Get it off me! GET THAT MOTHERFUCKER OFFA ME OH CHRIST OH JESUS YAAAHHHH—*"

But it wasn't just that voice or the sound of something being squeezed out like a dishrag full of soapy water that stopped Romero and Aquintez, it was a screeching, strident noise that echoed out, making the windows shake and rattle in their frames. It wasn't an animal sound or a human sound really, but maybe a little bit of both and neither. A raging, deranged shriek that faded into something like scratching black laughter, laughter filled with contempt and appetite and—Romero was thinking—a certain evil pleasure, a childish sound of glee.

Sure, that's it, he thought, *that's it exactly. Damon's on the loose and he's having a good time just like some wicked little boy lighting cats' tails on fire or pulling the wings off flies.*

Except it wasn't cats or flies...but people.

Damon's playthings.

Aquintez behind him, they made for the infirmary door at the end of the passage. It was ripped from its hinges. And tossed like broken toy soldiers and gutted ragdolls were inmates and guards, some alive, but most dead. Some of them were out of their minds, their eyes like shining ball bearings in the flashlight beam. They had seen something. Romero was sure of it and whatever it had been, it had sucked their minds dry, wrung out thought and memory and sanity in an oily slag that ran from their ears. They were mumbling and making empty sobbing sounds, staring blankly.

"Jesus," Aquintez said. "It wasn't like this before...it wasn't this bad. Something...I guess something must have happened..."

Outside the entrance to the infirmary, they found the body of a con.

His head had been nearly twisted from his shoulders, both arms snapped off at the elbows, and as a humorous gesture from a bored child, his tongue and everything that held it in place had been yanked out of a chasm below his chin where it hung like a pink and bleeding necktie. They stepped over him and, oh Christ, it was even worse inside. The infirmary was a long, narrow room like a hospital ward in an old movie and this one predated even the silents by nearly a century. You could see the looted drug cabinets and supply closets.

But that had happened before Damon went on his tear.

Now the walls, the beds, the ceiling were red with splotches and streaks of blood. There were bodies and parts of them everywhere. It was a study in ghoulish creativity and the mind of a jaded, degenerate child that knew no earthly bounds. Men had been dismembered. Men had been beheaded. Men had been skinned and plucked and disemboweled. Men had their bones pulled right through their skins and stacked in red, tidy heaps next to their boneless shells. Men were strung from light fixtures by ropes of their own viscera and their skins were tacked up over the windows with shards of bone driven into the plaster. A slaughterhouse and butcher shop and dissection room laid bare and ugly.

But there was one bed untouched.

One form sleeping beneath a crisp white sheet that was wet with slime, but not so much as a drop of blood had stained it or the man who slept there.

Palmquist.

Romero got close to him, close enough to touch. He found a flashlight on the floor and put it on him. The kid did not stir. His head was bandaged and the bandages were dyed red. Using Aquintez's penlight, Romero examined the kid's eyes. One of them was dilated like a black marble and there was no response from the light. The other pupil was the size of a pinhole.

"He's got a concussion and probably brain damage," Romero said in a weak voice, the stink of blood and meat and voided bowels choking him. "He could be in a coma for a day or two weeks and every night—"

That's when Aquintez screamed.

Romero felt something swing by him like a bell rope and then Aquintez was screaming. A pink tentacle covered with tumorous suckers pulled him right off his feet and into the air.

Romero put the light up there.

He'd brushed aside spiderwebs when he first got to the bed, but now he saw they weren't spiderwebs but wire-thin gossamer filaments of something connecting the kid and what was above him, spread over the ceiling.

Damon.

Romero let out a tiny, involuntary cry.

Aquintez was dangling up there, looped by Damon.

Palmquist's nocturnal brother was bigger than three bed sheets strung together. Just a roiling gray mass of tissue set with a coiling network of white, fibrous growths. Dozens of opaque tubes and feelers and bloated fleshy tentacles were writhing and snaking from that miasmic horror, roiling like flatworms and maggots and corkscrewing like the tails of hogs, searching along the ceiling and tapping the individual tiles like fingers.

It was obscene. It was positively obscene.

Romero stared at it, playing the light along its mass that reached out in every direction and seemed to be growing by the moment. Its tentacles were made of a gelid flesh that was transparent like the skin of deep-sea shrimp. Fluids flowed through veins and collected in capillaries. Some of the tentacles ended in hooks and others in black depressions like mouths that dripped an acrid juice.

Romero wasn't sure where he found the strength.

Outside, the war went on and on, but it was very distant like something heard playing from a neighbor's TV on a summer night. Quite calmly and lucidly, Romero said, "Damon, put the man down. You know my voice, you know you can trust me..."

The thing up there surged and squirmed, it flesh broke open with blisters that weren't blisters but flat yellow eyes set with red-slit pupils. At least two dozen of them and more opening all the time.

"Damon," Romero said, droplets of juice hitting him now and burning holes in his skin. He flinched, but did not waver. "Please, put the man down."

And of all the crazy, unbelievable things, the creature did.

It set Aquintez back on his feet and his mouth was locked in a crooked, silent scream, his eyes black as tidal pools.

Romero looked at the thing.

It looked back at him.

He tried to tell himself not to hate it, not to let his skin crawl and stomach boil with the absolute disgust and revulsion that it inspired. His aversion to it was more than physical, but spiritual. This then was the hidden brother, the externalized other, the crawling, creeping monstrosity that swam in the scummy pools and dirty, polluted backwaters of Palmquist's soul. A thing born of childhood terrors and nightmares, spawned in some invidious lagoon of primal human terror.

But Romero thought he maybe could control it.

Then something like a huge central mouth ringed with yellow curving fangs opened up and the beast that was Damon let go with a screeching howl of pure anger. It took Aquintez and pulled him apart, all those tentacles and tubers moving in him and through him, investigating and prodding and rending.

And that's also when Romero moved.

He pulled a shank from inside the back of his pants and put it into Palmquist's throat, sawed and cut until his hands were warm and wet with blood and tears ran from his eyes.

Oh, Danny, oh Jesus, kid, I'm sorry...

Damon dropped what was left of Aquintez.

He let out an echoing, bone-rattling roar: freight trains and tornadoes and cluster bombs and wailing sirens, an explosion of raw, shrill noise that put Romero to his knees, made his eardrums implode and his nose bleed and his heart seize up, filling him with a manic need to claw out his own eyes.

And then Damon fell.

Fell and blanketed Romero, wanting to crush and kill and squeeze and tear...but as Palmquist died, so did his brother. Damon came apart in a rain of filth and blood, scum and offal and squirming, squealing things and then was nothing but a slimy, gelatinous pool.

And then the lights came on.

What was left of Damon steamed and bubbled and evaporated.

Romero shielded his eyes as the SWAT team came through the door. Maybe they saw the carnage and maybe they saw the knife in his hand. Regardless, they did not hesitate.

Romero opened his mouth.

And about thirty bullets went through him, dropping him dead next to Palmquist's bed. He let out a final, wracking breath and died. And with what he had seen, it was almost a blessing.

The riot was over.

And so was Damon.

About the Author

Tim Curran is the author of the novels *Skin Medicine*, *Hive*, *Dead Sea*, *Resurrection*, *Hag Night*, *Skull Moon*, *The Devil Next Door*, *Doll Face*, *Afterburn*, *House of Skin*, and *Biohazard*. His short stories have been collected in *Bone Marrow Stew* and *Zombie Pulp*. His novellas include *The Underdwelling*, *The Corpse King*, *Puppet Graveyard*, *Worm*, and *Blackout*. His short stories have appeared in such magazines as *City Slab*, *Flesh&Blood*, *Book of Dark Wisdom*, and *Inhuman*, as well as anthologies such as *Shadows Over Main Street*, *Eulogies III*, and *October Dreams II*. His fiction has been translated into German, Japanese, Spanish, and Italian.

Find him on Facebook at:
https://www.facebook.com/tim.curran.77

Bibliography

<u>Novels</u>
Afterburn
Bad Girl in the Box
Biohazard
Blooding Night
Cannibal Corpse, m/c
Clownflesh
Dead Sea
Doll Face
Graveworm
Grim Riders
Grimweave
Hag Night
Hive

Hive 2: The Spawning
House of Skin
Long Black Coffin
Monstrosity
Nightcrawlers
Resurrection
Skin Medicine
Skull Moon
Terror Cell
The Devil Next Door

Novellas
Blackout
Corpse Rider
Deadlock
Fear Me
Headhunter
Leviathan
Puppet Graveyard
Sow
Tenebris
The Corpse King
The Underdwelling
Toxic Shadows
Worm

Collections
Alien Horrors
Bone Marrow Stew
The Brain Leeches and Other Eldritch Phenomena
Dead Sea Chronicles
Here There Be Monsters
Horrors of War
Zombie Pulp

Curious about other Crossroad Press books? Stop by our
website: http://crossroadpress.com
We offer quality writing
in digital, audio, and print formats.

Subscribe to our newsletter on the website homepage and
receive a free eBook.

Made in the USA
Las Vegas, NV
30 September 2023